UNDERNEATH
THE TREE

PRINCIPAL FUNDER

All proceeds from this anthology will be donated to the
Simon Community NI and World of Owls NI.

UNDERNEATH THE TREE

Twelve Christmas stories

from writers in Northern Ireland

edited by

Claire Savage and Kelly Creighton

Sesheta

First published in 2020
by Sesheta
Northern Ireland

ISBN: 9798672324098

seshetawords.wordpress.com

Contents

Introduction

Filled with a diverse collection of festive stories from writers across Northern Ireland, *Underneath the Tree* showcases just some of the great variety of talent we have here in the north. Included within these pages is an eclectic mix of genres from writers with a broad range of experience, all of whom bring their own particular styles and voices to the anthology. The result is a book which conjures up the magic of Christmas … along with the more spooky aspects of this seasonal holiday.

The idea for the anthology was first conceived back in December 2019. We thought it would be great to publish a collection of Christmas stories from Northern Irish writers, as it seemed none currently existed. It would also provide another platform for local writers to share their work and, during our planning, we decided the proceeds should be donated to charity, making it a community project through and through.

As such, all proceeds from *Underneath the Tree's* paperback and e-book sales will go to two local charities – the Simon Community NI and the World of Owls NI – both of which do wonderful work with people and animals throughout the province.

While the project ultimately ended up being put together during 2020's Covid-19 pandemic, it was not one which arose specifically out of lockdown. We had already set up Sesheta – a community organisation aimed at showcasing Northern Irish writing – and acquired funding from the Arts Council of Northern Ireland before Corona Virus reared its head.

That being said, however, the ongoing pandemic – and its impact on creative professionals in particular – just makes us even more glad that we got this project off the ground and have been able to support the Northern Irish writers who are included as part of it. The same goes for being able to help, in some small way, our chosen charities.

Underneath the Tree is a collection of festive tales that we hope you will enjoy reading over the Christmas period and beyond. We're delighted to bring you this selection box of stories from Northern Ireland and hope that you enjoy them as much as we do.

**Claire Savage and Kelly Creighton,
November 2020**

Candy Canes, Comics and Christmas

Gary McKay

I met Marlene atop Lily Hill on December 17, 1983, two weeks after my tenth birthday. The news of the Harrods bombing – the IRA's crime against Christmas – was all the talk in Ballykey that afternoon, but I was too young to understand. I'd popped out to get some sweets and, on a whim, decided to climb Lily Hill while the weather wasn't awful. This was one of my favourite places to read superhero comics in peace – at home, Ma told me I was filling my head with nonsense and at school, both the boys and girls teased me. It's grown in popularity in recent years as a tourist destination, but back then, not many people came to Lily Hill, which suited me just fine.

I didn't realise someone was already there until I rounded the final bend of the hill. It was a girl with short, blonde hair, dressed in a jumper and skirt. A necklace with a series of stars on it hung from her neck. I paused and considered retreating, but she'd seen me. The girl waved and skipped over before I could move.

"Hi!"

"Hi."

"I'm new in town."

I nodded, unsure what else to say.

3

"Do you like comics?"

She'd seen my Spider-Man bag.

Tentatively, I nodded again and waited for the insults to fly. I was tired of being told superhero comics weren't for girls, that I should stick to *Bunty*, Barbie dolls and unicorns. Why couldn't I enjoy what I wanted in peace?

The girl's face lit up with the brightest smile I'd ever seen – even her eyes seemed to glow for a second. "That's so cool! I love superheroes!"

My mouth opened, but no words came out. I'd never met another girl who liked superheroes and feared I never would – not in Ballykey, anyway.

"I'm Marlene, by the way."

"Annie."

"Pleased to meet you, super Annie!"

I grinned. No one had ever called me that before. I fished in my bag and pulled out a well-worn *Batman* issue.

"Do you wanna read this with me?"

"Yeah!"

We skipped over to a tree and spent the afternoon reading comics beneath it. I didn't have a best friend – had never had one – but by the end of that afternoon I knew Marlene was mine.

It was also the start of my most important Christmas tradition.

***

"What if Batman and Spider-Man got into a fight?"

Marlene and I were huddled over an issue of *The Amazing Spider-Man* in her room, listening to the rain beat against the roof – a typical summer's day in Northern Ireland.

I shrugged. "Spidey would win. No bother."

"Hmm."

4

Atop the hill, we took cover beneath a tree – the same one as in 1983 – and looked at Ballykey below, lit up like a budget Christmas tree. Marlene produced a candy cane from her bag and passed me one. We tapped them together six times and popped them in our mouths.

"Imagine if we had Wonder Woman's invisible plane, Marl. We could go anywhere in the world. Imagine Christmas in Australia – we could sunbathe!"

"Don't think gingers do all that well in Australia, Annie."

"Oi!" I laughed. "Maybe Germany then."

In the school library, I'd read about different Christmas traditions from around the world and liked the sound of Germany's.

"I think I'd spend all my Christmases here, if I could."

"In Ballykey?" I snorted in disbelief. "Catch yourself on, Marl – it's freezing, and nothing fun ever happens here."

"I like the cold and the quiet. It feels right for Christmas. Besides, hot chocolate wouldn't be the same if it was warm outside. I—"

Marlene coughed violently. Her candy cane shot out of her mouth and she doubled over.

"Marl!" I put an arm around her, cursing myself for not listening to Ma. "Are you okay?"

She took a series of shuddering breaths. "I'm okay, Annie." Another painful cough shook her body. "I'm okay."

Marlene wasn't okay. She hadn't been okay for a while. We'd been best friends for six years and until last summer, I'd never even heard her cough, despite her dandering around the place in all weather. Since then, she'd been plagued by a never-ending cold that seemed to get worse with each passing month. She'd had a good week – Christmas always brightened her spirits – but I should've known better.

"Marl, have you seen a doctor or something?"

She squeezed my arm. "It's just a cold. Don't worry."

"We should go."

"Not yet. Let's sit a wee while longer."

"Five minutes, then we're off – I'll carry you on my back if I have to."

"Five minutes."

I exhaled and watched the air waft away, wondering what sort of cold lasts for months and months. Surely her parents were worried? A sharp pain crossed my forehead and I winced.

"What're you getting for Christmas, Annie?"

I blinked. The pain was gone.

"Dunno. Probably comics and stuff." Ma's resistance to superhero comics had weakened since I'd met Marlene. I'd even caught her reading a *Wonder Woman* issue last year. "What about you?"

"Same, I guess." She relaxed against me. "I'm so glad I met you, super Annie."

"Magic Marl."

We sat together in silence for some time, perfectly at peace with the world and each other.

It's one of my favourite memories.

***

"I'm off, Ma." I shouted from the hall, to be heard above the kitchen radio. "See you later!"

"Wile early, isn't it?"

"I'm gonna meet Marl before school."

"Who?"

"Marlene!"

Ma opened the kitchen door. "Is that a new mate of yours?"

"What?" I was dumbfounded. "Marlene? Marlene Martin? My best friend?"

"I didn't think you had a best friend, dear."

"We … we ate chips here yesterday!"

Ma shook her head. "Aye, me and you did, but there was no Marlene there." She moved into the hall. "Are you okay, Annie?"

"Ma … are … are you on something?" She'd hit the bottle hard after the divorce, but as far as I knew hadn't had a drop in years. "You've not had wine, have you?"

Her face flushed red with fury. "Clear off, you wee shit, before I clip your ear!"

I fled out the front door and ran to Winell Street, where I was to meet Marlene.

She wasn't there.

***

Marlene wasn't at school either. They didn't even call her name during the class attendance check. I considered speaking up, but something stopped me. Instead, during break-time, I approached Shannon McKendry, who sat beside Marlene during chemistry, and asked if she'd heard anything about her.

"Who?"

"Marlene Martin."

Shannon shook her head. "Sorry, Annie. No clue who that is." Mock concern appeared in her voice. "Maybe you need Spider-Man to help you out, like. Could buck you while he's at it too."

Dazed, I wandered off, Shannon's shrill laughter ringing in my ears.

The remainder of the school day passed painfully slowly.

***

After school, with more fear than I'd ever known in my life, I ran to Glen Drive, where Marlene lived. She had to be there. The cold or whatever it was had gotten worse, and her parents had kept her off school. It made sense.

11

But why had everyone forgotten her?

I remembered last summer – the disappearing wall and what Marlene said to me as I was leaving.

One day I'm gonna up and disappear.

This memory recurred over and over in my mind as I ran, scaring me more each time, until I was shaking with fear.

Ten minutes after leaving school, I staggered to a halt on Glen Drive and looked for Marlene's house, number seventeen.

It wasn't there.

Glen Drive stopped at number sixteen and next to that was an overgrown field. I stared at it for several minutes, hearing the thump of my heart. First the wall, now the entire house. A scream was building in my throat. I clamped my hands over my mouth and breathed through my nose. Losing control now wouldn't help Marlene, wherever she was.

I looked behind me and my eyes widened.

Of course, where else would she be?

***

I climbed Lily Hill as fast as I could, falling several times in my haste, feeling like I was moving in a dream. The thought brought me to a halt, halfway up the hill. I'd been so swept up in everything, it'd never occurred to me this could all be some awful dream. I pinched myself hard and willed the world around me to fade to nothingness, but nothing happened.

I resumed climbing and, just as I had six years ago, rounded the final bend of Lily Hill and saw Marlene, dressed in a jumper and skirt.

I stopped dead. Marlene turned and smiled. Her cheeks and forehead were cracked like old porcelain and a yellowish-white light shone from the cracks. She groaned and clutched her chest.

"Marl!"

I ran towards her and halted just short of the light's reach.

"Annie." Her voice sounded strained, as if speaking required a great effort. "You came. I'm so glad."

"Marl ... what ..." I took a step closer. I'd expected the light to be dazzling, but it didn't even make me blink. "What's wrong?"

"My time's almost up."

"Don't be silly – you're only sixteen! We'll ... we'll go to a hospital." I took her hand. It was roasting. "Get you some help. The doctors will know what to do."

She shook her head.

"Come on, you can't just ..." I pulled her hand. She didn't move. "I can carry you. I ... please, let me help you. Please." I couldn't hold the tears back any longer and they fell in ugly sobs. "Marl."

"Annie." She reached a hand forward and touched my cheek. "Let's not waste this time. Sit with me. Please?"

I wiped my face on my blazer's sleeve and took a deep breath.

"Five minutes, then I'm getting you to a doctor."

"Five minutes." She sighed. "Yes, that sounds about right."

I helped Marlene beneath our tree and held her against me, despite the heat. Ballykey, still largely covered in yesterday's snow, looked the perfect picture of tranquillity. It didn't seem fair that anywhere could be at peace while Marlene was suffering, least of all Ballykey.

"I hoped I'd last until Christmas. It'd have been lovely to sing some carols. Oh, and the dinner." Marlene licked her lips. "I sure love brussels sprouts."

She coughed and her body trembled.

"Sure, you can have as many as you want." My voice wobbled. "Hundreds, if you like. No bother."

She shook her head.

"Why not?"

"Time's up."

"I don't understand!"

"I was never really here, Annie. Just passing through."

"What does that mean?" I thought of Ma and Sharon and Glen Drive, and shivered.

"You're right here." I squeezed her. "See? You're here and I'm here, and … and …" I pulled two candy canes out of my bag and waved them in front of her face. "Your favourite, look. And—"

"Annie, listen to me: I'm stardust, drifting through."

"What?"

"This is my Christmas gift for you."

Marlene touched my forehead and stars exploded into life around me – beauty beyond words. The universe was awash with colour against a black backdrop. I craned my neck to watch a comet zoom past, its core an eerie green, followed by a blue and grey tail that lingered after the comet was out of sight. I smiled, remembering last year, when Marlene, Ma and I had stayed up late to watch a lunar eclipse. We'd devoured a special midnight picnic beneath the full moon and eaten so much cake our stomachs were still sore the next day.

The images continued: wonders and marvels I'll remember until my dying breath, including a series of green stars that aligned themselves perfectly like a Christmas tree. Behind them, a sun exploded and was reborn.

Everywhere and everything was stardust, in the end.

Beautiful, perfect stardust.

The universe faded away, yet with its beauty had also come understanding.

"That was you, Marl."

Marlene nodded.

"I always wanted to know what it'd be like to have a life like this, on a planet. I passed many in my travels." She smiled. "Your loneliness drew me to you, Annie, and I couldn't have asked for a better friend."

"But you aged."

'Hullo,' he braved, taking in the scene of the neat kitchen, the range grown cold and table strewn with letters and dockets. 'Hullo,' he ventured again, louder this time and directed his call towards the stairs. When no response came, he took the stairs two at a time, a cold dread prickling his neck like the kiss from a czarownica, the whispering witch of his homeland.

He stopped suddenly on the landing, for there he could see reflected in the dark glass of the old mirror hanging above a washstand, a scene of awful savagery. A tangle of limbs, slick with darkening congealed blood, lay splayed on a patchwork eiderdown that covered the metal bed. It was a grotesque tableau that made him think of birth, butchery or war. His brain took a moment to reconfigure the image and he saw that it was a mother and her children, for there were two little ones, silent and staring, clutched together. He felt again the presence of the whispering witches of his people, but they were kindly beings, called on for healing and could do nothing for the creatures laid out on that death bed.

Later, Ivan and other men from the village found the husband, Artimus Becker, hanged in the barn. His was a neat death in comparison, yet it had its own imagery of the grotesque in the protruding purple-bruised tongue, the bulging eyes and cesspit stench of loosened bowels. They cut him down and had the priest conduct a prayer to stave off the daemons that had undoubtedly found their way into his heart.

The men hung their heads low and mumbled words of prayer with a suitable melancholic air.

One of them began whistling the bars of a low lament. Soon the voices rose up and the echo reverberated through the valley in a dull moan of an ache. The womenfolk stopped their chores and listened.

Later the priest referred to the bishop regarding the burial, for who could say if it would be right to bury them in consecrated ground? Hilda Macken asked where else would you bury the mother and her two children, and the menfolk looked at her like she'd walked straight out of the swampland with two heads. There were murmurs of rightness and wrongness and variants of grey in between. Hilda, Nancy and Ivan the Pole couldn't see this grey in-between light of which they spoke.

The priest interjected, his finger worrying at his collar, tightened like a noose at his neck, 'The father must have been under undue stresses with things we aren't privy too. This was not his hand that did the deed, but that of the devil himself, and sure who knows what goes on behind closed doors. The woman could have been mithering him and the poor soul was tortured beyond reason.'

The menfolk nodded. They knew of this mithering of which he spoke and could attest for how it could drive a man to do insane things. The women looked concerned.

It was decreed that the women would wash the bodies of the children and the mother. The man Artimus Becker would be lain out first and served with a proper gwylnos to keep vigil over the corpse. It was decided that there would be no keening and since no surviving family member could protest it was decided.

A linen cloth was hung over the mirror and the curtains were pulled across the windows to shield out the night.

At the gwylnos the village folk gathered to pay their respects and passed the funeral cake between them which was washed down with a sup of the warmed mulled wine. They wore their good black gloves and talked of the old days and the price of a good burial. The singing began low, but before long a four-part harmony rose up to wake the angels. A sin eater had been ordered to come forth from the next village and was presented for all to see. He approached the corpse laid out on the well-scrubbed table and dipped his piece of bread in the well of salt, sat waiting in on the depressed chest of the man Artimus Becker. Eating greedily at the fresh bread dunked into the salt and drinking down the mulled wine proffered, the sin eater provided ceremony and penance for the dead man. The priest elbowed the sin eater to remind him to say his bit. 'I give rest and easement to thee, for peace I pawn my soul.'

The next day the bell rang out and the villagers lined up to pay their respects as the dead bodies were carried, wrapped in their white mourning sheets, as the procession made its way to the church. A simple service was provided by the priest who led the worshippers in a hearty rendition of the hymn Gwahoddiad.

The women kept their mouths clamped shut. Gathered at the graveside on the far end of the church land, the grave digger raised his spade, rubbed the soil off it and offered it to those gathered. Before taking their leave, the village men placed a silver coin on the spade to stave off the time of their own death.

Allowances had been made by the bishop for the sake of decency and the family were buried together in the village graveyard.

In a plot at the far end of the field away from the church, but still within safe range of being on the scared ground they revered so much.

Hilda Macken and the womenfolk muttered their disapproval, for why should the poor mother, Efa Beck, be forced to lie for an eternity with the man whose hand had taken her life and that of her poor children? Their mutterings were only heard by Ivan the Pole and the child Nancy who both agreed.

The days blew in and before the village had time to grieve the loss of some of their own, Christmas Eve was upon them.

Hilda poked at the fire and watched as the logs settled into blackened sticks with molten orange licks. The old woman of the house had prepped the goose and the odd white feather rose and fell with the bluster of cold air meeting warmth.

Talk of Christmases past occupied them and before long Hilda mentioned the bad affair of the Becker family. The crog loft cottage had lay empty with its black cast iron pot sat on the range still holding the congealing remains of the family's last meal cooked.

'Perhaps it's time,' said the old woman. 'You'll be needing a place of your own soon enough.' Her eyes rested on her daughter's swelling belly and Hilda turned back to the fire her face flushed.

Hilda's choice of a man hadn't worked out well for her. Cadell had his habits and he liked to adhere to them as if his life depended on it.

His absences were explained as hunting trips but the rewards of a boar meat feast, more often than not, occasioned a mere rabbit pie. A cottage of her own might be preferable to having the rheumy eyes of her mother watching his every failing.

On Christmas morning Hilda woke early, fed her child and went about her chores.

Her mother fussed about the child, scrubbing its cheeks until they pinked and dressed it in its good bonnet. Hilda dressed herself in her Sunday best for the church service but made sure to put on her good sturdy walking boots.

She had slept on the old woman's suggestion and thought it prudent to give the Becker family's crog loft a once over, before putting the plan in to action. If she liked the cottage, she'd put it to Cadell over the evening dinner. A feed of goose and a bottle of stout would surely place him in a good humour. She considered how men were often more superstitious about these things than women. Hilda had noted the practicalities of raising a family often fell to the woman. The men liked to make a show of presiding and providing, whereas the women quietly birthed, fed and cleaned. Hilda had started to wonder at this, and it ruminated in her mind like a festering scab waiting to be picked at from time to time.

The Christmas morning service ended with a hymn and a candle lit in remembrance of the Becker family four. Hilda bowed her head and whispered to her mother that she'd be home in an hour, she'd an errand to run.

The old woman said nothing for she knew her daughter better than the girl knew herself, and happily walked the two miles home with the grandchild in her arms thinking on the crog loft about to be claimed.

When Hilda reached the lane that approached the Becker cottage, she started to find the scent of turf smoke lingering in the cold morning air. The crog loft looked abandoned and lonely against the blue frosted valley, yet there was something not right about the scene. Hilda chided herself for being romantic and given to whimsy. The scent of turf must have drifted from Ivan the Pole's neighbouring house. She peered in through the cottage window and saw the unlit oil lamp sitting on the cwpwrdd gwydir. How handsome the cupboard looked with its glass fronted doors. Hilda liked the idea of placing a few books behind the glass and some good crockery if she ever was to own some. She could imagine herself baking some bara brith in the range and settling the new babi in a basket in the corner. By spring the firstborn would be toddling and she'd have her hands full, but the thought of it made her smile.

With a breeze at her neck Hilda wondered at the last moments of the Beck mother, Efa. Had she cowered and pleaded or fought with all her might? Did she know what evil lurked within the man she'd lay down with at night? Hilda couldn't help thinking that it would be wise for any mother to know the value of a well-placed poker, should the occasion arise. She chided herself for such dark thoughts but knew she'd rise to the challenge should the instance ever require it.

She pushed on the cottage door and it gave way easily enough for who was there to lock it? When the worst that could happen occurred within the croft's own walls, fear and safety had no purpose. She stepped inside and at once noticed the warmth within the room that by rights should not be there. The slate floor looked freshly swept and the scent of sweet bread hung in the air. Hilda was certain she was not alone. She sensed rather than saw the family in the house. Later when the old woman pushed her on it, she could give no details, just to reiterate that there were two girls sat at the breakfast table and the woman, Efa, was at the range. It was true that she hadn't seen it with her eyes, but she had felt it deep within her soul.

'And the father, Artimus where was he?' Cadell had asked.

Hilda shrugged. She knew where she believed him to be – in the spitting fires of hell but she knew that the menfolk wouldn't want to think on that.

The next day, Gwyl san Steffan, was celebrated in the usual way with the tradition of holly-beating or holming as the elders called it.

The young men of the village gathered with boughs of freshly picked holly to beat the unprotected arms of young girls until they steaked with crimson slashes of blood.

The girls laughed and screamed in delight until it dawned on the smarter of them that the tradition wasn't as fun they'd been led to believe.

Later they bathed their lacerated arms and vowed among themselves to not engage in the ritual the following year. Things could change they said, if they wanted it to. They thought of the dead Efa Becker and her daughters too.

27

Talk went about the place as talk does, and the village women made it known that the croft was to remain as it was, untouched. Hilda chose to stay with her mother until a more suitable abode was found and, in the spring, when her boy child was born, she moved further up the glen. She kept Cadell under a watchful eye and felt certain if he didn't attend to her needs and that of her children, he would meet a misfortunate. The mother Efa Becker had left lessons for them all.

By the following November the villagers gathered to remember and pray for their dead. Bad times had come to the valley. A collapse in the pit had killed a man from almost every family.

Hilda had lost Cadell though to be true she neither mourned nor missed him. Those who were left, Ivan the Pole and the few others from up the glen were known for their advanced ways of dealing with women. They neither scolded not patronised, promised nor threatened.

This modern way was shocking to some, but the dearth of men led to a new way in the village. The women were seen for their worth of character rather than any old ways of being judged on the assets owned by their father, or the bounty of their pretty looks. Life continued for those who remained and new habits were formed.

Hilda and the little girl Nancy visited the Beck croft often, leaving a posy of sweet-smelling flowers on the door stoop or a sprig of lavender on the windowsill.

No high-pitched screeching noises nor ghostly sightings were reported, but the feeling was that the mother Efa Beck had refused her burial place alongside her murderous husband and taking her daughters with her, had returned to their croft to see out their eternal days as spectres. The Beck croft stayed as it was for the pleasure of the three dead female inhabitants and the villagers paid their respects with gathered clutches of flowers and sweet-smelling herbs.

The seasons changed, and when Ivan was the last man standing, there was talk among the women as to how they could change the run of bad luck. The men for all their trouble where useful and necessary for the future of the village. Their talk went around in circles – 'We must ask the Gwyllion fae folk to bless us with more men.'

'But what is the point if they are to only be driven to their graves?'

For the next few nights Hilda struggled to find sleep. She tossed and turned and when she eventually found rest she dreamt of bog swamps with a sensation of sinking into the land.

On the third night, she woke with a start and a terrible sensation of a heaviness pressing down on her. She struggled to breathe and tried to get up but found the impossible weight holding her prisoner in the bed. Eventually the dead weight left her, and she drifted off to sleep again. When she woke in the morning, she had a clarity of vision as to what needed to be done.

Ivan the Pole accompanied Hilda to the spot and soon all the remaining villagers, mainly women and girls with the odd boy child, gathered to watch. Ivan braced himself and began digging.

By noon the remains of Efa Becker and her two murdered daughters were removed from the clutches of the murderous Artimus. Settled in a freshly dug grave, lined with sweet herbs and wildflowers from the valley, the Becker women could rest in peace.

Now at Christmas time, when families gather around the hearth, or at least those who remain, the story of the Becker family is told as a fair warning. For it is known that a shared grave should not be the final resting place of a wronged woman, since the scared plot cannot hold a righteous wife laid down with her murderer on top.

The man near the bus stop

Stuart Wilson

The night was cold, he felt the frost in the air and his feet had crunched on the thin layer of snow that was on the ground. The darkness of the night was broken by the hiss coming from the streetlights and the glow of decorated trees in various windows in the houses, the soft wind moved the trees that lined the road in front of him. 'It is a leafy suburb at Christmas time, you can't miss it.' He now smiled at the description that he had been given. He had been to this city before, but he had never been to this part, but then, he had never needed to before. He pushed his hands deeper in the pockets of the thick outdoor jacket, the small woollen hat covered most of his head, he lowered his face into the upturned collar of the jacket, nearly obscuring his face as he sat motionless on the bench.

His feet were warm in the boots he had brought with him, but he was regretting wearing jeans, the cold went straight through them.

Behind him only the trees moved in the unlit park as the wind made them creak, whiffs of snow were picked up by small cyclones and drew lines in the crusted snow on the ground as they danced around the park.

The row of detached houses along the street were each surrounded by their own trees and hedges. All the houses were large and Victorian by design but looked to have been built in the last twenty years.

They all had gravel covered driveways that led up to large front doors with ornate furnishing, the windows were designed to look like Victorian design, but the brick and stonework gave it away that they were not. Each house had a small selection of expensive cars and they all faced onto the park, although most were in darkness now. It was a far cry from where he had been raised. He was from the opposite end of the spectrum, he wanted to hate them, but part of him could not. His mind wandered; what kind of people lived here? What jobs in the city did they do? If they saw him sitting in a coffee shop would they speak to him or just ignore him?

He had been sat there for a while, waiting, no one had spoken to him or even taken any notice of the non-descript 'man near the bus stop' who had been walking around the park just after sunset but was now sitting on the bench. Each would later say they were not sure of exactly what time he had arrived. He had been careful. He knew which of the houses had CCTV and security, he had avoided showing his face to them. He had easily found the house he was looking for. The address and description had been precise. The white front door with the large number on it, a Christmas tree in the window to the left of the door with an angel on top and not a star like most of the Christmas trees in the street. The black Range Rover and the dark green Aston Martin that were parked outside the front door and never in the double garage that was attached to the side of the two-storey red brick house. He had memorised the registration numbers of both, it was just another confirmation that he had the right place. Now he sat, on the bench, motionless, waiting.

Across the road and down to the left was the small bus stop. He had drawn every line of the shelter in his head to pass the time:
the shape of the shelter, where the dark green paint was flaking off, the posters in the frames that were mounted on the back of it.

The covering that extended a few feet out towards the road that would give some cover from the earlier snow and the small row of red plastic seats that were so uncomfortable that no one ever sat there. They were too high for most to sit on, you had to mostly just lean against them, but they were there. There was no shelter from the wind.

He did not have to look at his watch, he knew it was almost midnight, he did not want to move, he did not want to expose his wrist to the cold, but he had to sit there, waiting, and time was moving slowly, but still he would wait.

His eyes looked up at the clouds that covered the sky without moving his head, the roar of the engines of an airplane above the clouds had drawn his attention, he tried not to let the small smile spread across his face as he looked at the clouds, he had seen that type of cloud many times before, it was going to snow again. He knew what types of clouds would bring rain, what would bring snow and of course, the type that held in a thunderstorm that would make him need to seek shelter.

His eyes caught the movement of the cat from around the tree to his left. His eyes darted over to the movement. The cat slowly walked from the far side of the tree, deliberately pacing as it moved towards the road. It stopped. It looked over at him and he looked at it and they both paused before the cat broke off the stare and slowly moved off towards the bus stop. He watched it as it padded its way around the bus stop and reappeared at the far side then turned around, sat down and looked back at him. He smiled. For a moment, he thought the cat had smiled back at him.

He drew the cat in his head, the shape of the body, the light-coloured fur with the dark markings down their side and the way the markings moved as the cat walked, where the tail lay on the snow. The cat had made no sound, nothing, it was the movement that had attracted his eyes.

33

The cat moved like a true hunter. He studied the face of the cat, the round face had the small triangles on top for ears. The cat obviously had whiskers, but he could not make them out from where he was. The cat blinked and looked around where it was. He looked around where he was sitting, apart from the wind and the cat, nothing was moving, he felt the cold trying to bite in through the gaps around his neck, he settled down again, as did the cat.

His eyes were drawn over to his left, he heard them before he could see them, the laughter, the noise of their movement as they came crashing out of a garden further down the street. Two were teenagers but the third was older, but not by much. The two teenagers had small rucksacks on their backs, and they were moving quickly, laughing as they did so, they had just come out of one of the houses and they were loud, very loud. He looked directly at the house, expecting windows to be filled with light, but none did. He sat still, only his eyes moved, they had not noticed him.

They came around the bus stop and the older one spotted the cat. He had a thin tracksuit top over an old fleece, his jeans were dirty and it had not been washed in a while, his hair was dark and unkempt, personal hygiene was not a top priority for the leader of the small group. The other two were the same, unwashed, unkempt and unruly, he knew the type, he had known them all of his life, the normal rules of society did not apply to these, they could do whatever they wanted to and no one could stop them, they did not have anything, so they would take, from whatever and whoever they pleased and they would feel right in doing so. He despised them already, but still he did not move.

The two teenagers spilled out on to the road, they were all heading towards the park behind him, they were in a very good mood and were keen to get away from the house they had broken into.

34

"Hey look!" shouted the older one as he pointed towards the cat. The cat did not move, it looked at him, but before it could do anything the older one kicked with his right foot as if taking a penalty in a game of football, a kick so fierce that it launched the cat up and into the rear of the bus stop.

The cat had made a noise of pain before the collision with the hard surface stopped it.

The cat fell onto the ground and landed in the snow with a flop. It did not move. The cat was dead. He looked up at the three laughing males, his eyes focused on the older one as they turned and started to run towards him.

"That was brill, did you hear the noise it made!" one of the teenagers shouted as he laughed, all three suddenly stopped as he stood up. They had not seen him until he had moved, his hands were still in the pockets.

"Why did you kill that cat?" he asked quietly. His accent seemed like it was Eastern European, he was certainly not from around here, the older one stepped towards the middle of the road, closing the gap between them.

"What is it to you? Prick! Was it your cat?" He went from laughing to aggressive, the others followed their leader, guessing something was about to happen, and there were three of them. They looked at the man who was on the bench, he was much older than they were, this would be an easy fight.

"No," he had lowered his voice, "it was not my cat." His eyes looked into the eyes of the older one, then quickly glanced at the other two before staring at the older one again as he spoke, "but it was someone's! It had a collar on." The older one looked over at the other two then slowly started to pace toward him, the other two did the same.

"But who cares!" he was almost shouting, he had raised his arms as well, it was then that he spotted that the older one had a small folded knife in his right hand, his eye darted over toward the other two, they had started to fumble in their own pockets, he guessed looking for knives of their own.

35

"It was only a bloody cat!" the older one continued as he lowered his arms.

"It didn't deserve to die." He had a stern look on his face as the three of them came closer.

"Well, it's none of your business anyhow!" said one of the others.

The youngest one spoke, "Yeah … and you can just piss off back to your own country!" He was answered by approving calls of 'yeah' and 'right on' but still the only thing that moved were his eyes.

"So, what were you doing in that house?" he asked.

"Dropped in to wish a former teacher a 'Happy Christmas'," the older one stated.

"And gave his missus a 'special' Christmas pressie for all three of us!" one of the teenagers spoke and finished off with a ghoulish laugh that the other two after sharing a glance joined in on.

"But," the third one started. "What we did with her is none of your business, right!" He opened the blade as he spoke. The three looked at each other and shared a laugh and followed in unison by blades clicked into place. Whatever had happened in the house, they were proud of. The teenagers reached the pavement, the older one continued to slowly walk towards him, he now moved the blade in front of himself as if he was cutting through the air.

"And I don't like it when people stick their nose in my business!" he glanced at the other two for approval, "don't like it at all," the older one was smiling as he spoke.

The man turned, stepped around the bench and started to walk away from them and towards the darkness of the park. "HEY!" the older one shouted, the man turned and looked back over his shoulder at him.

"You didn't have to kill the cat!" he spoke quietly but loud enough for them to hear.

36

"Who gives a toss about the cat?" one of the teenagers remarked, the older one had a stern look on his face, the laugher had gone.

"Hey," he said as he nodded towards the man. "What have you got?" The older one had reached the pavement now.

"What have I got?" the man asked as his body started to turn back towards them, he glanced down at the grass under his feet then looked back at the three of them again.

"Yeah... What you got in your pockets?" The older one nodded as he spoke, "I want your wallet, your phone and anything else you have in there!" The man remained emotionless as the older one continued, "also, what's the pin for your cards?" His intention was now fully clear. One of the man's arms moved and his right hand came out of his pocket. None of them could have guessed he would have a small pistol. There was a spitting noise as the man extended his right hand towards them, the first the older one knew something was wrong was when a great force hit him in the face, his body spun, he could not see that the other two had already fallen and dark pools had started to form around them, colouring the snow on the ground, all three bodies lay still.

The man looked around where he was, he lowered his right arm, the thumb on his right hand moved up and flicked the safety catch on the small pistol. The metal tube attached to the front of it ensured that the noise it made was no more than that of someone spitting. He adjusted his jacket and replaced the pistol back in his pocket.

He slowly looked around the ground and spotted where the three empty bullet cases were lying. With slow deliberate movements he walked over and picked them up, dropping them in the same pocket as the weapon. His eyes moved over the three dead people lying on the ground contorted, steam rose from the red liquid that was still seeping onto the cold ground. The steam would stop soon as the heat from the bodies was taken by the cold night.

As he walked back towards the bench he looked around, there was no one to be seen, nothing moved in the quiet street.

He lifted his jacket up and reached into the right-hand pocket of his jeans, it was a bit of a struggle but the phone he had been given popped out eventually. He opened the contacts and clicked on the only number that was there. The screen of the phone lit up as the number rang. His eyes looked up again, his head gently moved from side to side before looking back at the screen. The call would not be answered, he already knew that. The call was cut from the other end, they had got the message. He put the phone in the same pocket as the pistol and sat back down on the bench. Silence returned to the street. He looked at the watch on his wrist, it had just gone midnight. He turned slightly and looked back at the three bodies on the ground.

"Merry Christmas!" he exclaimed. He sat forward again and replaced his hands back in the pockets of the jacket. Time passed slowly again, so he waited. Motionless. His eyes looked over at the cat. Outwardly he did not move, but his eyes moved over the lifeless body, the way it lay on the ground. He could not see its face, the legs pointed away from him, he could see its back and tail, its fur gently moved by the wind. For a short moment he mourned the poor creature. The sound of a car made his eyes look to the right and up the street of trees and parked cars.

The car pulled up on the road and stopped opposite him. The driver looked at him as he stood up. As he walked over towards the car, he unzipped the jacket and slid it off his arms. The passenger door opened as he approached. He wrapped the jacket and its contents into a ball which was tossed over the top of the passenger seat into the rear of the car. The jacket and the contents were now someone else's problem, he would not concern himself with it again. He instantly felt the warmth of the car as the door closed after him and he got comfortable in the front passenger seat.

"Well?" the driver asked.

"No one is home," he replied.

"Another time then," the driver remarked.

"Yeah, probably." He shrugged. He reached forward and increased the heat coming form the car, he would be warm soon enough.

"Who are they?" the driver asked. The man looked out the passenger window at the three bodies, then looked at the driver.

"No one that matters!"

"Ok." The driver shrugged before he looked around. "Will you still need the flight tonight?" the driver asked. He looked at the driver and did not speak. He turned his head and looked out the windscreen.

"So, the target wasn't home then?" the driver asked, he glared at him, then looked back out the passenger window.

"You are paid to drive the car, not ask questions!"

The car moved off down the street and the two of them carried on in silence. The topic of the flight would not be raised again as the car slowly made its way down the snow-covered street.

Will She Remember the Lights?

Samuel Poots

The reader spits out my finance card, its screen flashing a book and cross in luminous green. The young man behind the counter gives me a wary look as he hands the card back and says, in a carefully neutral tone, "Sorry, Brother, your account has been locked."

His words ripple through the queue of people behind me, their stares prickling across my skin like crawling ants. All I can do is murmur an apology, hoping that I sound more confused than guilty, before hurrying out of the store and making my way to the Financial Office across the town square.

Winter winds have stripped the place bare of people. Even the Security Deacons have found excuses to linger indoors, which is one small mercy.

The only other face I see as I cross the open span of concrete is that of the Reverend Father shining from his pole-mounted projectors. The image flashes from fatherly love to stern disapproval, so I'm never quite sure which I'll see when I look up. Normally, I take some comfort from the sight. Light blazes from that face, pushing back the growing shadows of this darkest time of the year.

It might be a far cry from the colourful bunting of my childhood, but I take pride in knowing that it's often my wiring that keeps the Reverend Father always before us.

Normally.

The doors to the Financial Office slide open and a small, dumpy woman in a grey jacket and skirt looks up from behind her desk. She smiles in a cut-glass kind of way. "Hello, Brother. Peace be with you. How might the Church help?"

"I appear to be locked out," I say, proud that I can keep my voice from trembling. What if they've made me an *Invisible*?

She plucks my card from my fingers and feeds it into her own account reader. The machine whirs away to itself and she frowns down at the screen as all the little secrets of my financial history play out before her. It's all I can do not to try and crane my neck to see.

My breath starts to come in little gasps. The more I try to control it, the more panicked it grows.

I feel the urge to flee, to go home, grab Cynthia and never stop running, though I don't know where we could run to.

Which is stupid of me! I haven't done anything wrong. Not even the slightest disloyalty to the Reverend Father.

Not to the Reverend Father, maybe, whispers a voice in the back of my thoughts. *But what you're planning is hardly in keeping with his message, is it?*

Before I can stamp that out, the reader gives a little bleep and the woman breaks into a grin. "Well, Brother Graham, you'll be relieved to hear that you're not locked out as any sort of punishment."

"I'm not? I mean—" I hurry on when she raises an eyebrow. "Of course I'm not. I just meant, well, it's not that I did anything or … What I mean is, why are my finances locked then?"

She lets out a silvery laugh. "Oh, it's quite routine at this time of year. We carry out random financial blocks throughout the parish, just to make sure no one is trying to bring back any of those old, unholy ways." Her smile practically glitters at its edges. "It's as well to be vigilant. After all, if one day is declared holy, does that not mean others are made less so?"

Almost verbatim from the Reverend Father's *First Sermon on the Purity of Worship*. A low sigh of relief escapes between my lips and I'm already reaching forward for my card when she continues.

"I just have to ask you a few questions and then you'll be free to make your purchases. Is that all right?"

She hits a button on the computer, quite oblivious to the fresh panic she's sent spiking through my chest. "What were you planning on purchasing today?"

"Craft supplies. Coloured ink and the like." Which is true. "For my daughter." My palms tingle at the tacked-on lie.

"As a gift?"

"No. No, certainly not. School project." A painful lump builds in my throat. My eyes wander to my finance card sticking out the back of the machine.

It would be so much easier to just talk to the Reverend Father; I'm sure he would be an understanding man. But I have yet to earn the right to meet with him, despite all my work. Such honours are reserved only for those who have proven their devotion through labour and dedication. So the Church Elders tell me with each day's list of tasks.

"One final thing," the woman says. This time she looks up. Her eyes are as cold and distant as the sky outside. "Will you be attending special service on the twenty-fifth of this month?"

I almost let myself relax. "No, of course not. Just the usual sermon broadcast."

Silence stretches out between us for a long second. I wish I could see what she has typed for the Church Elders. My palms keep tingling, clammy, no matter how much I wipe them against my trousers. There aren't any other doors I can see, but that doesn't mean that Security Deacons aren't about to rush in declaring judgement upon me, that they haven't somehow read my mind and seen the Tree.

The reader beeps once more and my card is spat out half an inch, ready to be taken.

"That all appears to be in order, Brother." The woman gives another of her glass-sharp grins. "The Church has been quite generous with your funds, I see."

I take the card, resisting the urge to turn and run with it out into the street. "I helped with the meeting house wiring. Lighting, you know?"

"Doing the Lord's work," she says with a nod. "You have a good day now."

The glass doors slide open behind me letting in another grey-suited figure clutching their finance card in one tight fist. The wind, once bitter, is now almost refreshing, blowing away the fear of the Financial Office. I hurry off to make my purchases, not looking up at the flashing expressions of the Reverend Father in case I see the wrong one.

I can vaguely remember the days when those images didn't sit atop their poles. Winter would come and the whole town would be strung about with colourful threads of light, all spelling out Merry Christmas, and the shops were full of toys no one could afford anymore. It's all little more than flashes of colour now, dulled by time to just a sense of the occasion. I have no idea why they used to decorate trees like that and when I was old enough for such explanations to matter, there was no one around to tell me. But I do remember how it made everything feel special.

It's good that it's gone, along with all those other trappings of a time that forgot God.

Before the Church took it all away and led us back to economic and moral well-being.

But four-year-olds don't think about those things. They see the lights and know something special is happening.

My Cynthia's the same age I was then.

I have to step over an Invisible to get to my car. I'm glad to see the paint hasn't been scratched. The Church only gifted me with it a month ago so I can help fix the electrics at meeting houses around the county. I point it for home, while above the town looms the familiar symbol of the closed book behind a blood-red cross.

***

I walk to the forest. It's not that I'm ungrateful for the car, but I'm fairly certain it's tracked. It would be silly of the Church not to keep an eye on its property and I know the Elders wouldn't understand what I'm doing. If I'm honest, I'm not entirely sure that I do either.

Dusk gathers quickly at this time of year, leaching all colour out of the world. By the time I reach my chosen tree, there isn't much light left to work by. It stands at the centre of a cluster of other pines, each one reaching up to the sky, branches intertwining with one another to form a great domed cathedral. Compared to those, the one I've selected looks pretty unimpressive. You wouldn't think it was special at all, but for one little girl I hope it will become a memory she can hold onto.

I unload my electrical tools and craft supplies and get to work. Every so often, a stick snaps or a branch creaks and I pause, not daring to breathe. Security Deacons don't have much call to be out this far from the towns, but you never can be too sure. Their zeal for the Church is … inspiring.

I don't continue working until I am sure it was just an animal and try to ignore the growing prickling feeling on the back of my neck.

45

It's slow going, but fortunately there isn't much left to do. I'm finding a quiet satisfaction from this project, far more then I get just endlessly re-wiring the meeting house's old television set. When the last strand of bulbs is hung from the branches, their glass dipped in colourful inks to tint their light, I step back to admire my work.

"And God said, 'Let there be Light' and He saw that the light was good."

I don't mean to speak the words. They bring a little sting of shame with them, a minor blasphemy – the sort that the Reverend Father warns can build up one upon the other like snowflakes, until all the world is swept away by an avalanche of small transgressions. For a second, I want to tear down this thing I've made and fling it back into the distant past, where the Elders have rightfully confined it. But I can still remember the wonder of those mornings, still remember the feeling of seeing a tree light up a room. And I want Cynthia to have that.

Behind me, something rustles in the underbrush. I freeze.

Any second there'll be a yell, a heavy hand on my shoulder, a Security Deacon reading out the rites of banishment and driving it home with their club. I strain my hearing, waiting for that next sound.

Another soft snap of twigs. Could they be sneaking up behind me? But the Security Deacons don't sneak. They're the glorious arm of the Reverend Father's will. They don't hide who they are, they declare it for all to know that their time for repentance is now passed. Another animal? But I've never heard any that move with that measured tread.

I spin around, ready to run at any sign of—

It's an Invisible. A woman, dressed in an assortment of rags, looks back at me from behind a tree. Her eyes glimmer in the shadows, two bright points in the fading day.

We stand there for a long time. A second figure appears beside her, their ragged clothes also marking them as an Invisible. Then a third.

The whole world grows distant and still as they watch me and I watch them.

I turn my back on them and set off as fast as I can walk. I should report them. Three in one place – and confident, too, to show themselves. Maybe they live there, in the forest. Invisibles are not allowed to make settlements. They must wander forever, never stopping, never resting, doing penance for whatever wrong caused the Church to cut off their finances and banish them from all decent society. Everyone who touches them, who even looks at them, is made unclean and must share their fate.

No money, no friends, no family, no Church. Just endless wandering, driven on by the Security Deacons.

I should report them! But then the Church would find the Tree. Would one good deed outweigh the crime?

I walk alone except for my thoughts and the moon emerging high above, the Invisibles' eyes shining bright in my mind.

***

Cynthia is playing alone with her dolls when I come to collect her from crèche. The roughly carved figures were lent to us by the Church for her birthday, each one a little replica of someone from our perfect society. The Mother. The Father. The Child. The Reverend Father. The Security Deacon.

She has removed the little floral-print dress from the Mother and put it onto the Security Deacon, who looks quite fetching in that and a bulbous green helmet. I smother a smile. The Church would definitely not approve.

She holds the doll up for inspection.

"Look! She wanted to be a Security Deacon too, so she can fight bad guys. And now all the others want to watch her fight a ..." She frowns for a moment and then grins in triumph. "A croco-cow!"

I know I should be disapproving, but despite myself, I laugh. If I'm allowed my little transgression, maybe I should allow her this one. I scoop Cynthia up into my arms. "A croco-cow? What's that then, little 'un?"

She inspects her dress-clad Security Deacon. "I dunno. But Sister Francesca at school showed us a picture of Noah's Ark and there was a crocodile on it, but it looked like a green cow, so I think that's a croco-cow. With big, *big* teeth!" She demonstrates by making gnashing gestures with her hands.

After being eaten by the croco-cow, I put her down and tell her to get her coat. "We're going for a little trip before we go home."

"Can I bring my dolls?"

"No. Don't want to get them lost. But make sure to put on your gloves, it's going to be cold out there."

We have to risk the car. A December night is no time to make a four-year-old walk all the way out to the forest. Hopefully, whoever tracks Church cars will have better things to do then worry about us taking a half-hour trip out to the forest. In her seat beside me, Cynthia is singing one of the songs they teach at school.

"Watching over, watching over, He is watching over me. Watching over, watching over—"

She's got stuck on the chorus, trapped in a joyous little loop of her own. I don't have the heart to tell her to stop, but those words press down on me, growing heavier with each new repetition. I mutter an apology to God and pray to Him that the Reverend Father will be understanding too.

The forest is crisp and cool, a fresh rime of frost crunching beneath our feet. I keep Cynthia quiet during the tramp up to the Tree by the simple trick of giving her a boiled mint sweet.

She's still sucking on it with a curiously determined expression by the time we reach the spot.

"All right," I say, letting go of her hand. "Wait right there, love."

"It's dark out here."

"Don't worry, I'm going to switch a light on."

"Forests don't have lights and I don't like it!"

"Just a minute, pet, just a minute and I'll – aha!" Searching around at the base of the Tree, I locate the power pack I'd smuggled there. With a flourish she can't possibly see, I flick the switch.

The quiet of the forest breaks as the power pack chugs, whirs and hums itself into life. And then ... then there is light.

Cynthia's jaw drops open, the mint slipping from her tongue. She's not alone. I can't believe what I'm seeing. On every branch, woven between the great strands of lights I had set up myself, the Tree has been adorned with all manner of colourful decorations. They sparkle against the dark green, looking so rich and vibrant that it takes me a minute to realise they've been made from junk.

On one branch a brown and red robin hangs, its feathers made out of old scraps of cloth. On another, a star made from twists of tin-foil spins gently. Here, a paper angel, there a twig reindeer. On their own, each thing might appear shoddy. Together, on our Tree and with my lights, it is a sight from Christmases of childhoods past.

At last, Cynthia breathes. "Daddy, it's a light tree!" She looks up at me and now her grey eyes sparkle as bright as any light I could make. "Did you make it?"

"Well, some of it," I admit. And that's when I spot the dark shapes lurking around the edges of the Tree's halo.

They step into this arboreal cathedral in ones and twos. Ill-fitting, much-repaired clothes hang from wire-thin frames. Most of them are young – there's rarely such a thing as an old Invisible – some barely more than children themselves. And all of them have their hollow-eyed gaze fixed firmly on our Tree.

There must be a dozen of them! I hold Cynthia close to me and try to keep all the Invisibles in sight at once. How can there be so many people who have rejected the ways of the Church?

"Who are they, Daddy?" Cynthia asks.

"No one!" I snap without thinking. "No one. Don't look at them, love. They're not people anymore."

"But they're putting more stuff on the tree. Look!"

Sure enough, some of the Invisibles are carrying more of the lovely, scratch-built decorations. They dangle them wherever they find a space, covering it in Christmas. One of them turns and I recognise the woman from earlier.

She smiles and starts walking towards us. I push Cynthia behind me, away from her.

The woman has a hand extended, her lips opening, about to speak and I clap my hands over my ears, not willing to hear whatever blasphemies she might say.

Something tugs at my sleeve. "Daddy, she says I can hang this one up. Can I?"

The Invisible is crouching in front of Cynthia. And my little girl is holding up an angel with wings of golden sweet wrappers. The Invisible smiles again at me. The expression looks strained and for the first time I realise how – well, how rude I must look standing in front of her with my hands on my ears.

I start to shake my head, but then a thought catches me by surprise. After all, I had wanted to show her what Christmas was like when I was a kid. Why shouldn't she be allowed this one?

The woman leads my daughter to the Tree. She lifts Cynthia up, making my little girl giggle. With the solemnity of an ancient ritual, Cynthia sets the angel in its place. The moment stretches out around me. It's like my awareness has expanded and I can see us all, Cynthia and me, all these people, gathered together in a little island of light.

A loud bang cuts through the night. Something hisses into our midst. Then a blinding flash sears the world in shadows.

People yell. I can't see, my head is ringing. Frantically, I call for Cynthia, reaching for her, arms flailing everywhere. The world has turned into Babel as everyone yells at once.

From somewhere there comes a crack. Then another and another and another and another. Each one is like a butcher's cleaver sinking through meat to find the chopping block. Cries of pain are abruptly cut off. And I still can't find Cynthia.

Something is bundled into my arms and I feel the comforting weight of my daughter. She's crying, calling for me even as she's clutching at my coat.

"Go!" someone yells in my ear. "Go, now!"

I don't argue. Holding Cynthia tight to my chest, I turn and run. Shapes start to emerge from the blazing after images, shadow blobs that could be people, could be trees. I just focus all of my energy on running. Running as far and as fast as I can.

To either side I can hear others shouting. Some are the Invisibles, screaming in pain and fear in a way I could never shut out and ignore. Others are the sharp, barked commands of the Security Deacons, demanding everyone get on the ground by the word of the Reverend Father!

My lungs begin to burn. I try to force my legs on, muscles screaming at the effort, but I know I can't keep this up. In my arms, Cynthia is beyond tears. She hangs there, her little heart beating so fast that I can feel it even through her thick winter coat.

Vision is leaking slowly back into the world.

Lights flash through the trees, white beams cut to ribbons by their shadowy trunks. I want to look back, to see what's happening – see if anyone is chasing us. My head starts to turn.

No! Mustn't look back. Might trip and fall. Might turn to salt. Just run!

But I can't run anymore.

Stumbling to a halt behind a tree, I let myself slide to the ground. I rock my little girl in my lap and vaguely try to shush her, murmuring comforting sounds that don't quite manage to be words.

Footsteps sound somewhere close, but I don't have the strength to try and get away. In my arms, Cynthia shivers.

They grow louder, coming closer. I know I won't let the Security Deacons take her. No matter how tired I am, no matter that they are the Reverend Father's own and wear the cross and the book on their sleeve, I won't let them take her. I tense my whole body, ready for whatever comes next.

The woman, the one who had held Cynthia up to the Tree, sprints past. She doesn't stop, doesn't even see us here, tucked away in the forest's shadows. She runs with her head down, intent on just getting away. Which is why she doesn't see the Security Deacon as he looms up out of the gloom. His baton connects with her skull with a sickening crack.

Cynthia jerks. I look down to see her staring in horror as the man leans down to start cuffing the woman. I put my hand over Cynthia's mouth, gently, just to make sure. We stay silent as the man throws the Invisible over his shoulder, lugging her like a sack of potatoes back in the direction of our Tree, where even now the sounds of panic are beginning to die.

***

We don't go back to the car. I can't be sure if the Security Deacons were tracking it, or if they had been planning on breaking up that group of people before we ever got here. I'll have to report it as stolen. Instead, I steer us back to the road by a longer route, carrying Cynthia the whole time. My head is full of thoughts I can't quite fit into words, weighing the rest of me down. Images from the forest keep playing out in front of my eyes, no matter how much I try to shake myself free of them.

Cynthia is quiet. I'm not sure what to say to her. I mean, what she saw – she's only four and I took her into that and she heard the shouting and the people being beaten and yelling to one another, people who had decorated a tree with us. Will she even remember the lights?

"Daddy, you're squeezing too hard."

Her little voice brings me back. Slowly, I lower her to the ground and take her hand. "Sorry, little 'un. You all right?"

She nods and we carry on side-by-side and, though I can't see her clearly in the gloom, I can't sense any fear from her. It's like the bad things are behind us and never happened, but I know these silences of hers, the ones that mean she's thinking hard about something.

At last, she asks, "Why did the bad guys do that?"

"Those weren't the—" I stop and take a deep breath. "I'll talk to you about it later, pet. But you can't go talking to anyone else about it, all right?"

She nods, but how much can I trust in the promise of a four-year-old? "I mean it. If you say something and someone learns we were out there, then – then the bad guys might come to our house."

Cynthia gives this some further thought. "Don't worry, Daddy," she says. "I'll make the bad guys go away."

What can you do except laugh at the simplicity of that? "Thank you, pet. I feel much safer already."

This was a stupid idea. I never should have done it. And all for what? To try and recapture something that ties us to those heathen, materialist ways?

But for a moment, her world had been full of light. And I can't help but smile at the thought of her standing there before the Tree, eyes sparkling with the lights I put there for her while all around, others place yet more glittering pieces on the branches to make the Christmas tree shine even brighter.

"Will we go see a light tree again next year?" Cynthia asks.

I can practically feel her gaze on me, those big, grey eyes that only hours before had shone with the lights of the Tree. And something inside me breaks. "Yes," I say. "Yes. Why not?" I think for a moment and then add, "But maybe next time, we'll find a way to hide the lights more."

"Under a bushel." I glance down at her. She looks surprisingly solemn for a four-year-old child. "That's where Reverend Father says you hide a light. Under a bushel."

All I can do is shake my head.

We walk the rest of the way in silence. Back home and then on to the meeting house where the Reverend Father will be preaching to the faithful from his television set.

The Thirteenth Hour

Claire Savage

Yvaine scanned the horizon. The moon owned the sky this Christmas Eve, adorning the countryside with a subtle silver glow. Tonight, she was a full, fat orb, suspended in a clear sky twitching with stars. For those abroad, the night nipped at their heels as the hour drew on, the earth cooling and compressing with each passing second.

For Yvaine, the moonlight was unnecessary, an extravagance that she was not reliant upon but which, she conceded, didn't exactly encumber her when she was on the hunt. In truth, however, she preferred to be swaddled in darkness. She tilted her head, focusing on the myriad rustlings and scurrying sounds below. She listened to the breeze as it ruffled the grasses, distinguished the snuffling of badger from the foot-falls of fox.

Bats nipped to and fro in the gloom, their high-pitched sonar bouncing off bark and insect and mammal. She sensed the movements of a shrew, then a pair of field mice, as they tip-toed from their fortified burrow, limbs still heavy with sleep. A ribbon of river whispered against banks pock-marked with hidden dwellings, its soft speech punctuated every so often with murmuring ripples as an otter, water vole or rat slipped into its cool depths.

Tonight, however, Yvaine did not seek prey. There were festivities afoot and she fully intended to join them. She just needed to discover their location first.

With the night wrapped up cold, it sharpened her senses and, feeling content, she took a moment to groom her feathers – bronze and caramel dappled with smoky grey. Her face was pale as milk, as was her underbelly, and the overall effect was that in flight, her appearance was eerie and ghostlike. She flexed her talons, eyeing the hooked points that would fail to skewer flesh until the moon retreated.

Fresh movement below made Yvaine pause in her preening. A shiver passed through her and she searched for its source. Her head turned towards a great gnarled oak and, as she stared intently, she saw a cloud of effervescent mist tumble down its cracked trunk. As it descended the timber in silence the mysterious frothing mass began to separate, spilling down the bark like the tears of the moon herself.

Eclipsed by curiosity, Yvaine waited and watched, safe on her perch, as the fizzing forms flowed to the ground, moving across it like a stream of stardust.

Indeed, they left in their wake a shimmering trail, as if a giant slug or snail had passed that way, winking in the light of the sixpence moon.

Yvaine finally took to the wing, keeping her eyes trained on the apparitions as they continued to grow and gain definition, transforming into lithe, sinewy beings as they danced and skipped below her. The translucent shapes soon became bodies with tiny torsos and pinched waists, limbs thin as twigs unfurling into hands and feet that moved with nimble grace and were as slim as toothpicks. She could snap them easily.

Their ears elongated, stretching to fine points, while their candyfloss hair streamed out behind them as they raced onwards; on others, it stood up in messy tufts, or framed angular faces like storm clouds.

From their backs (Yvaine noted each knobble of spine) gauzy appendages unfurled into wings long and tapered, fine veins spider-webbed across their surfaces.

With each stage of their metamorphosis, the creatures' bodies took on more solid outlines, albeit ones edged in electric silver, their voices growing stronger and clearer. It was a language that tonight, Yvaine could understand. They chattered about their Midwinter gathering and a special task they had to complete, though there was no mention of what exactly this was.

Some clutched pipes and flutes, while others carried harps and one, a twisted horn. They flaunted themselves in the moonlight and their boldness captivated Yvaine.

They skipped on and she followed.

***

The tingling they felt from the barn owl's unwavering gaze was as deliciously infuriating as a tickle. Her heart-shaped face was a second moon in their sky and they delighted in it as their procession trooped towards the enigma of the thirteenth hour.

***

In the breath of time between Christmas Eve and Christmas Day morning it was known, mostly by those beings who dwelt within wood and hedgerow, forest and field – above ground and below it – that a gift was bestowed upon all beasts. Indeed, during the thirteenth hour, all animals had the power to communicate freely and legibly amongst species, even with humans, though very few people realised this, or were ever around to hear them. People, however, came in all shapes and sizes and one never knew who was afoot at such highly energised times of the year.

Tonight, a truce also held between predators and prey as this year, Winter Solstice aligned with Christmas Eve, adding to the potency of the date.

It was a rare occurrence for the two events to coincide and so, pro-offered an especially sacred space within the season to celebrate Midwinter, uniting the animals even more keenly as they gathered to mark the turning of time, ahead of lighter days. It also meant that tonight, a queen would be crowned in honour of the goddess – the moon – and all eyes would be watching to see whom she would choose.

It was an honour, of course, to be singled out by the moon, but she was a temperamental entity and took offence at the tiniest slight. Rudeness would not be tolerated, nor any other behaviour that she found unsavoury. She could bestow her favour, but she could also just as easily show contempt.

The coronation took place only when Christmas Eve collided with Yule and few whose hearts beat in anticipation tonight had ever been alive to witness it, nor knew how or where exactly it occurred. Instinct, however, drew them towards the forest where, ironically, the moon's glow barely penetrated, though they felt her unwavering presence in the sky, regardless. Instinct guided them on – that, and a subtle silvery trail imprinted upon the ground by invisible, pattering feet.

***

Yvaine glided above the starry procession like a mute banshee. The creatures' voices were like wind chimes as they sang lilting melodies and danced in time to their pipes and flutes, never straying from their path. Their cries and whoops rose up to where she flew, threading through her feathers – sneaking into her innermost thoughts and inviting them to waltz.

—

She moved her head slowly, from left to right, trying to shrug off their advances, but their grip was as fatal as her talons when they tore through flesh. She heard the distant chime of bells heralding the thirteenth hour and felt herself yield to its invitation.

Normally, Yvaine retreated during daylight hours – once dawn broke and the shadows that shielded her succumbed to a honeyed glow which spread into every nook and cranny of her night-time haunts, polluting them with light and uncloaking their secrets. However, she was not averse to hunting beyond the night, if food was scarce, though she much preferred to slumber until dusk.

In the thirteenth hour, Yvaine felt that she was in neither light nor darkness, entranced instead by a living path of spectres who emitted an unnatural ghostly glow as they meandered through field and scrub and into forest.

All she heard was the sound of their singing, all she saw was the crocodile shape of their procession. The forest swallowed them whole and blotted out the moon and still, she followed, for she knew, now, they would guide her to the Midwinter gathering.

***

This Christmas Eve there was no snow, only the beginnings of a thin frost which crackled like popping candy beneath paws, the winter chill tickling furred and feathered bodies but not quite penetrating their fluffy defences. The air was cool and clean, sharpened with fresh pine, and the warm-blooded procession regurgitated it in pale puffs of carbon dioxide which drifted away into darkness like beheaded dandelion clocks.

The magpies were in perfect dress for winter, their distinctive monochrome plumage particularly striking against the bleak landscape. Their inky feathers revealed subtle hues of iridescence when they caught the moonlight, painting them even more of a spectacle. Their hearts fluttered a little too quickly tonight, however, for they had their own secrets and, unbeknownst to the myth-makers and storytellers, they had no love of jewels or sparkling objects.

A magpie queen would just not do.

Zora muttered to herself as she and her family entered the forest.

"If we're celebrating the moon, couldn't we do it somewhere we can actually *see* it?" she asked, dodging a branch before it snagged her wing. "I hate these dark, enclosed spaces."

"Don't we all, Zora?" said her mate, Darkwing. "But it's tradition. If we honour the moon tonight, *especially* tonight, it will bode well for the new season to come."

"I know, I know," said Zora, swivelling her eye towards him. "And I know it's the safest time of the year to venture into this gloomy place, but that doesn't mean I have to like it."

"She's just worried in case they crown *her* the festival queen," said a young magpie. "Then she'll be decked out in finery and be jittery as a bed bug."

"Any one of us could be crowned," snapped Zora. "Or any one of *them*." She glanced to the animals moving across the forest floor beneath them. "It's an honour to be chosen, just not one *I* particularly wish to have. But if it's the goddess's will, then I'll succumb to it."

"But who *are* 'they'? Who'll actually crown the lucky beast?" piped up a badger ambling just behind their parliament. His voice was gravelly but with a strong timbre. "Even *I* have never seen a coronation. It's been many turns since Winter Solstice partnered with Christmas Eve."

"They say that it's done by special messengers from the moon," said a passing buzzard.

"Not by a natural beast, anyway," said a brown hare, as it joined in the conversation.

The magpies slowed their flight to listen, fanning the wintry air with elegant inky wings. They looked almost spectral themselves, with their snowy chests and otherwise shadowy plumage. Here, however, the moonlight failed to rest upon those iridescent feathers. Here, they remained dark as the night they now travelled through.

"Don't hares have some sort of affinity with the moon?" asked Zora. "Mightn't the goddess choose one of *your* kind?"

"Perhaps." The hare inclined its head. "But she has a mischievous side to her, the old tales say, so perhaps she'll select a beast less obvious than us and have some fun with her chosen queen this night. It could be any one of us."

"And what happens once the queen is crowned?" chipped in a robin, darting down to hitch a ride on the badger's broad back. "What happens then, eh? Does the moon keep her? Release her? Give her tasks to do in service to her?"

"That I don't know," said the hare. "But I suppose it all depends on what sort of mood the goddess is in and whether the crowned one pleases or displeases her. Surely it would be an honour to serve the moon in perpetuity though, bedecked in finery for her pleasure and our blessing?"

Zora said nothing and the magpies flew on.

***

Silence hung like a veil, draping over the animals as they made their way further into the forest's belly.

Perhaps that was why they chattered so, or perhaps it was simply because they revelled in using their fleeting talent of conversing easily with those not of their own kind, on this eve of Christmas.

Of course, they communicated across species in their own unique ways throughout the rest of the year, leaving spoors and tracks, scent markings and various other subtle clues that staked territories and warned others off.

They knew how to be invisible when danger lurked, when to shriek and scold and when to take to the wing or to run. It was difficult to shake off these behaviours which were so ingrained within their natures – so vital to their survival.

The younger creatures, who had lived through fewer seasons, therefore adapted more quickly to the change and were a little less rigid in embracing the festive truce and open lines of communication, consequently being more receptive to the excitement of the night. They tasted a fresh type of freedom on their tongues and were keen to make the most of the experience. For the more mature beasts, there was a need for easing slowly into the occasion, though they too still felt a frisson of elation, even if they wouldn't necessarily admit to it.

In the depths of the forest, the frost had yet to fully grip the branches in its icy embrace. The air smelled of damp, cold soil and mulch mixed with pine and the minty aroma of ground ivy, the pungent scent of juniper adding a tangy, woody undertone. Up until now, the season had been milder than expected, a confusion of plants clinging on into December when really, they should have retreated into the earth weeks ago. This displacement would continue on into spring, the wiser animals knew. There would be late flowerings and also, early appearances, if the winter continued to toy with them, turning cold then growing unseasonably mild before catching them all up in arctic chill again.

These days, it was harder to stay in step with the world.

***

Yvaine flew deeper into the forest, the tips of her wings brushing against branches that shivered in her wake. The trees grew more thickly together the further in she travelled, gradually forcing her lower and lower until soon, she was soaring within a whisper of her guides' heads.

***

The animals assembled at the heart of the forest, circling the periphery of a glade where the moon once again bathed everything in her lunar glow, all waiting in anticipation for the main event, which they sensed was growing ever closer. Badger and fox stood shoulder to shoulder, along with rabbit, hare, otter and stoat. Most beasts from the locality were represented in one form or another – some had come in pairs, others alone. Some, like Zora and her family, had flown in en masse, decorating the branches overhead like ominous baubles. Raptors perched beside drowsy songbirds who, for one night, had no need to fear their hooked talons and sharp beaks, though those nearest the birds of prey fluffed up their feathers a little more vigorously, cocooning themselves in soft familiar comfort.

A few sleepy squirrels had tucked themselves into the crooks of branches, curious, but keen to return to their cosy nests. All were perhaps not equally invested in the occasion but nevertheless, appreciated the gravity of it.

A blessing from the moon was not to be missed and none wanted to invoke her wrath.

And so, they waited and, after some time had passed, the sharper-eyed amongst them picked out a pale form flying towards the gathering; others detected the scent of warm blood overhead, while a few caught the taste of something in the air that they'd never sampled before – cold and otherworldly.

Others still were simply distracted by the sight and sounds of an odd procession that was singing songs of stardust and dreams and dancing its way ever closer to the beasts, who self-consciously drew back into the shadows around the glade as they approached.

**

The ethereal beings danced into a clearing where the scrawny branches of a willow wept to mossy ground, encircled by firs that prickled with unblinking eyes. The little party weaved in and out of the toadstools that sprang up to greet them, before finally settling down upon the cool, dewy moss – lithe, bony backs resting against the fungi.

Orbs of light wobbled into view from between the tightly packed trees, suspended briefly like detached, featureless heads, before darting across this secret place, trailing tongues of firelight in their wake. The flames floated above the little troupe, before an unseen force sucked them in like an octopus recoiling its tentacles, plunging them to the earth and igniting a bonfire of red and gold; green and blue.

It sparked and spat as the flames rose higher, filling the glade with smoky rainbow-coloured bubbles that popped against the pines, spilling a perfume of rose, magnolia and honeysuckle mingled with wood-smoke, moss and magic.

Unbroken in her flight until now, a drowsiness enveloped Yvaine and the owl fluttered her wings, spiralling down into the creatures' company and – she sensed – that of various other beasts besides. She felt many eyes upon her but her focus was solely on the tiny assembly of figures, who acknowledged her, at last, with peals of laughter that settled lightly upon her feathers and swept away all traces of every night she had passed before, bewitching her with their mirth – possessing her with their confetti-like caresses.

They stroked her plumage with cold skeletal fingers and peered into her black button eyes. A couple even perched upon her back as if she was a carousel pony.

They draped her body in pearls of moonbeams, scattered stardust upon her talons so they glittered like enchanted scythes. Through her wings they laced strings of diamonds and finally, upon her head they placed a tiny crown of gold, inlaid with sapphires, pearls and emeralds – at its heart, a ruby, reflecting.

Their touch – soft as snowflakes – sent tremors through her bones and Yvaine dipped her head in acknowledgement.

Coronation complete, the pale apparitions began to writhe as the pipes played once again, the music rising and falling as they contorted their fragile frames into impossible shapes, jumping and somersaulting and celebrating their feathered Yuletide queen.

They lay yet more gifts at her feet – necklaces, silks and gems.

A mirror.

Yvaine picked it up, her talons clutching the heavy silver handle as she raised it to gaze upon her face. She stared into the looking glass, utterly still, her eyes dilating. Frozen for a heartbeat – or perhaps, an eternity – the owl appeared to the watching beasts like a beautiful statue or a piece of precious art, enraptured.

The music died and silence smothered the glade.

Then Yvaine opened her beak and a screech rent the air, shattering the mirror. Slivers of glass sliced into luminous flesh and scattered fragments decorated the ground like fallen stars. Yvaine drew the gifts towards her, fanning her wings over them as she would her children.

She hissed and the sylphs hissed back.

Pulling at their hair, they shrieked as they ran towards her in rage, wrenching feathers as well as jewels from her body.

Struggling to escape their flurry of blows, Yvaine beat them back with her wings, showering pale pointed faces with pearls and diamonds – ripping tears in gossamer wings before taking to the air and plunging into the forest and out of the forest and up into the sky pregnant with a moon who frowned at her with motherly disapproval. She shook off the last of the glittering gems – watched them plop into the river below.

When at last she reached her hollow, dawn was whispering its arrival as the soft glow of the sun put an end to the moon's revelry. Songbirds roused themselves for the dawn chorus, those who had witnessed the coronation singing all the more merrily as they welcomed in the day – and Christmas Day, no less.

On the ground, the last of the animals who had attended the ceremony returned to their homes, where sleep would blur the memory of the night and soften its jagged edges. They would remember the excitement and the jewels perhaps; the silver creatures and the owl. A queen, crowned, then gone.

Perhaps they would think about a Midwinter blessing bestowed, then … well, who really knew?

The magpies chattered loudly as they retreated to their roosts. They would remember more, but would not speak of it except amongst themselves, for magpies were great secret-keepers and cleverer than most. They knew when to keep silent.

Yvaine huddled into the furthest recess of her home, cocooned in musty dark, the smell of oak and moss mingling with the scraps of forgotten flesh and bones; pellets carpeting her lair.

Her heart still thundered but her pulse gradually slowed into a steady beat.

Her head was heavy and she bowed it for sleep.

A tiny three-point crown of gold tumbled into the darkness, inlaid with sapphires, pearls and emeralds — at its heart, a ruby.

Rocking Around the Christmas Tree

Eddy Baker

Staring at the fireplace, Arlie was momentarily transfixed by the soft, flickering orange flames and the gentle crackling of the burning logs. She was enjoying a rare moment of tranquillity, the house empty but for the family cat snoozing peacefully on the hearth rug before her. Gazing deep into the flames as they danced and twisted around the wood, Arlie found herself fascinated with this act of consumption, the fire able to devour and destroy just about anything thrown its way. She looked down at her lap – at an address book open at the first page – and the pile of blank cards and envelopes either side of her. They'd make perfect fuel, she thought for a fleeting moment.

Arlie was snapped back into reality by the loud '*clack*' of the front door unlocking and the intrusive shudder as it opened inwards, filling the house with the noise of the outside world.

"*Arlie!*" yelled Marc, sounding somewhat out of breath and flustered. "The sheets, Arlie!"

Arlie cursed to herself and jumped up from the sofa, as cards and envelopes cascaded onto the floor. She grabbed the pile of old bedsheets she was supposed to have laid out long before Marc's return.

"Thanks a lot," huffed Marc, a spike of sarcasm in his voice. Arlie threw the sheets down in front of him, onto a floor already littered with pine needles. Marc dragged the huge tree into the hallway, Arlie pacing ahead of him to lay down further sheets. She'd insisted on this practice after last year, which had seen her spend several January days hoovering up pine needles from every corner.

Jake skipped past his parents and merrily giggled at the performance: Daddy grunting and puffing as he dragged the tree, Mummy yelling at daddy to "Wait!" or "Go!" as she adjusted sheets on the floor.

Eventually, the tree was in the lounge and erected onto its stand, to the gleeful applause of little Jake, who seemed delighted by the haggard monstrosity of a tree his father had chosen.

It was the only job Arlie had given Marc and true to form he'd half-arsed it. She'd given him specific instructions of which garden centre to go to and which type of tree they needed. Of course, she could have gone with him, or gone herself to choose it, but why should she?

It was early December and she'd already: set up the Christmas decorations, bought the presents, chosen the wrapping paper, planned Christmas dinner to the minute, ordered the turkey, sorted a date for Marc's parents to visit and handmade Jake's first Christmas stocking. And there was still plenty more to do. She'd sent Marc out to pick up the tree with Jake, just so she could have a moment of calm. Yet even then, she'd remembered the Christmas cards needed doing.

Marc's excuse for this mess of a tree was that he'd seen a sign on the dual carriageway directing him to a place selling them at a quarter of the price of those Arlie had sent him to. He'd ended up at some farm in the middle of nowhere, buying a creepy-looking, faded old pine.

"Think of the money we've just saved, that's more for you to spend on the rest of the presents," said Marc. Arlie bit her tongue and collapsed back onto the sofa, reaching down to gather up the piles of cards and envelopes once again.

"What are you doing?" Marc yelped. "It's no time to relax now, we need to decorate this baby!" Jake applauded in agreement and watched as his father up-ended a bag of tinsel, baubles and fairy lights onto the floor. Arlie smiled at Jake before explaining to Marc that she needed to get the cards done, as she wouldn't have any more free time to do it before the last Christmas post. Marc shrugged and got to work grabbing handfuls of tinsel, studiously approaching the tree with the thoughtful expression of a sculptor about to set to work on his magnum opus.

Sometime around the thirtieth envelope, Arlie looked up to see an incoherent mess of tinsel and baubles, with a noticeably lopsided arrangement of fairy lights. But she decided not to say anything, having already been made to feel like the killjoy enough for one day. And besides, soon afterwards she was able to enjoy a hit of schadenfreude, as the cat suddenly became enraged by an errant strand of tinsel and nearly brought the entire tree down. Marc did not see the funny side of this, chasing the cat out of the room as Jake and Arlie howled with laughter.

***

The next morning, Arlie was in a slightly brighter mood, feeling a little guilty for her initial reaction to the tree. It was still a horrendously ugly thing, possessing a creepy, spindly quality that unnerved her, but she had seen how much Jake enjoyed the whole ritual of choosing it and bringing it home to decorate. He was now sat in his high chair in the kitchen, chattering away to himself as Arlie made breakfast for the three of them.

Marc was absent, probably in the garage tinkering with his pushbike, ignoring his wife's calls for him to come and eat.

Eventually, Marc marched into the kitchen with a somewhat affronted expression. "What was so wrong with the green tinsel, exactly?" he asked.

"Sorry?" Arlie retorted.

"The tinsel. I could tell you didn't like me putting that green tinsel on the tree, but you could have told me instead of just taking it off the damn thing!"

Arlie had no idea what he was talking about. She paced into the lounge and, sure enough, the (absolutely, undeniably ugly) green tinsel Marc had added to the tree the day before was gone.

"That wasn't me," she protested, but Marc simply threw his arms up and strode back into the kitchen. Arlie stood for a moment, alone, gazing at the tree.

"It was probably the cat," said Arlie as she returned to the kitchen. "You saw what he's like with tinsel. We'll probably find it all buried in the garden a week from now."

Marc grunted through a mouthful of cereal and glared at his newspaper.

***

A couple of days later, Arlie stole herself another moment of peace, curling up on the sofa with a glass of wine while Marc and Jake played football in the garden. It had been a hectic few days, involving last-minute present shopping, wrapping paper disasters involving an over-excitable cat, and an incredibly stressful trip to the supermarket, during which Jake started a screaming fit over Arlie's refusal to buy him a box of breadsticks he had suddenly decided was all he wanted in the known world.

The fireplace was lit and again, Arlie found herself drifting off into a daydream, the flames once more twisting and flickering their hypnotic dance at her. She let out a low, pained sigh. Even when she tried her hardest to relax, she still felt somewhat on edge, always ready to spring up and turn her attention to whatever job needed doing next.

She envied Marc's carefree ability to wander in and out of their family life, disappearing to work on his bike one moment, reappearing to play 'Dad of the Year' with Jake the next. All she ever seemed to do, she feared, was be grumpy and say no to things. Arlie frowned, annoyed at herself for feeling so adversarial towards her partner. It was Christmas. A time for love and for family. She needed to snap out of this.

As if on command, something *did* snap her out of her train of thought, as she suddenly noticed movement in the corner of her eye. It was the tree – specifically, one of its branches, which was waving back and forth. "Fucking cat," she growled to herself and sprang up off the sofa, ready to seize the animal before it completed its assault on the tree. She stopped dead in her tracks when she realised the cat was still fast asleep in front of the fire, curled up in a ball and in no state to be launching assaults on anything. She looked back to the tree, which was perfectly still.

***

The following morning, it was as though Arlie was paying penance for daring to take some rest the day before. Jake had been up most of the night, complaining on a near-hourly basis of nightmares and monsters. For most of this Marc stayed asleep – or did a professional-level impersonation of someone fast asleep. Arlie stared zombie-like into her coffee as Jake ran excitedly around the kitchen.

He had all the energy of a child who hadn't spent the entire night screaming and wailing about beasts under his bed. Marc munched loudly on his toast in between bursts of a monotonous rant about fellow cyclists. Allie wasn't listening, but then again she wasn't entirely sure Marc was talking to anyone but himself.

Later on, Marc brought some bike parts into the kitchen, laying them out on the table and explaining to Arlie that he needed to make some adjustments and the light in the garage was too poor, and could she please pick up some bayonet top lightbulbs – 60 watt – the next time she was at the shops. Arlie left him to his tinkering and went to the front door to collect a handful of Christmas cards that had arrived. A few from aunts and uncles. One from her parents over in the States. One from Marc's work, which was addressed to 'Marc and Allie'. Jake scuttled past her and ran into the lounge, apparently pretending to be some variant of a velociraptor, eagle or bear; she wasn't sure which.

Suddenly there was a thud, followed by a brief pause and then a long, screeching wail from Jake in the lounge. Arlie ran in to find her son sprawled out on the floor near the tree, crying hysterically, an egg-shaped bump already forming on his forehead. *"The tree!"* he banshee-screamed. *"The tree pushed me over!"*

"What's going on?" yelled Marc, who had appeared at the lounge doorway.

"He fell over," said Arlie, picking Jake up and stroking his hair reassuringly. "He'll be okay, just a nasty bump. Ran into the tree, I think."

"Right, okay. Well, maybe he needs to calm down a bit, no? I'm trying to work in there and he's making a hell of a racket," said Marc as he wandered off back towards the kitchen. "And by the way," he called over his shoulder. "Don't think I haven't noticed you removed more of that tinsel!"

74

"The tree pushed me over," sniffled Jake, pointing accusingly at the Christmas tree, which was still rocking from their collision, a single branch waving silently in their direction. Arlie frowned at it, before kissing Jake on the forehead.

***

"You're looking so well!" said Ann as she handed her coat to Marc, embracing her son warmly. "And you too, Arlie, of course," she added with a smile, as she kissed Arlie on both cheeks. David shook his son's hand, then gave Arlie a quick peck on the cheek and followed his wife into the lounge.

"That ... is an interesting tree," stammered Ann when confronted with the increasingly twisted, dark pine before them.

"I picked it," said Marc proudly, before gesturing a thumb at Arlie. "She's not too much of a fan though." A sharp honk of laughter from David and Ann. "Well, I think it's lovely. Very unique. Very *you*," said Ann with a grin, jabbing a forefinger at Marc's chest. He chuckled and gestured to the sofa.

The in-laws safely seated in the living room, Arlie left them to catch up with their son while she prepared cups of tea and a platter of sandwiches.

She wondered if a frilly pink pinafore would be too on the nose right about now, but swallowed her misgivings. They'd only be here for the afternoon and then gone, she reminded herself. It had taken some doing, but she'd managed to convince Marc this year to keep Christmas Day just for the three of him.

"Such a shame we won't be here for Christmas Day," Arlie could hear Ann saying, in that bleating, whining tone she put on only for special occasions such as this.

Arlie grabbed the tray of sandwiches and hot drinks and entered the room as Ann continued, "We'd so love to spend the day with our grandson, wouldn't we, David?" David emitted a vague snort of agreement, although his attention was increasingly taken by the gnarled form of the Christmas tree in the corner.

"Where did you *find* that thing, Marc?" he asked his son. Arlie jumped in, "You should've seen the magic beans he got with it." This elicited another honk of laughter from the in-laws, with a slightly less enthusiastic chuckle from Marc. He shot her a slightly hurt look as she placed down the tray and handed out cups of tea.

"Arlie," Ann started. "We were just saying, it's a shame that we're not coming this year for—"

"Leave it, Mum," interrupted Marc, through a toothy smile. Ann stopped herself, smiled back then stared down at her tea.

"Hey," said Marc. "I'll go and get Jake for you, he's probably waking from his nap about now."

He bounced up from his seat and jogged upstairs. Arlie found herself sitting in awkward silence with Ann and David. She was about to speak but David broke the silence first.

"Lovely sandwiches," he mumbled through a mouthful of bread and tuna. "Absolutely," said Ann, nodding enthusiastically. "You've done really well." Arlie forced a smile with such vigour that she feared her face would start creaking.

"And how are you finding it since you stopped working?" asked David, only to receive a jab in the ribs from Ann. Arlie was about to answer when Marc strode purposefully into the room with a sleepy-looking Jake in his arms. He offered the dazed toddler around for hugs and cheek-squeezes from his grandparents.

As Ann and David marvelled at how much their grandson had grown, how long his hair was and all sorts of other measurements of progress, Marc sat beside Arlie and gave her hand a gentle squeeze of support.

"Oh my, what's this?!" exclaimed Ann, brushing back Jake's hair to reveal the egg-sized bump on his forehead.

"Oh, that. That's nothing," said Arlie, her in-laws now staring at her with mouths agape with concern. "He had a little fall yesterday, but he's fine."

Ann crinkled her forehead, almost brushing off Arlie's explanation as she cooed and fawned over Jake. "You poor little dear. That is a big *big* boo-boo, isn't it?" She turned back to Arlie. "Arlie, I know it's a busy time of year for you, but you really must keep an eye on him better. At this age they get themselves into all sorts of scrapes."

Arlie opened her mouth to respond, but felt Marc's grip tighten on her hand, a sort of pleading, warning squeeze. She kept her mouth shut. It was just for one day. No need for a repeat of last Christmas.

An afternoon of platitudes, DIY conversations and advice on Christmas dinner passed without too much incident and soon it was time for Ann and David to be on their way. Arlie had long come to expect at least one minor drama per visit and today was no exception, as Ann loudly complained upon getting up, that her scarf had gone missing. Neither Arlie nor Marc could recall seeing it, but Ann insisted she had placed it on the wooden chest next to the tree. Marc promised they would have a good look in case it showed up and gently ushered his parents towards the hallway, in the direction of coats and a merciful exit. They exchanged pleasant enough farewells, although Ann did make a show of tearing up as she kissed her son and grandson goodbye.

After Arlie had read Jake his bedtime story and tucked him in, she ambled downstairs, poured herself a glass of sherry and sat, exhausted at the kitchen table.

Tomorrow was Christmas Eve and she had to be up early to collect the turkey from the butchers, then take Jake to a nativity play performance at his nursery and then start the hours of prep for Christmas Day dinner. She'd asked Marc for some help peeling and chopping the various parsnips, carrots, potatoes and other elements forming the ludicrous feast on which he had insisted.

Marc had used the get-out clause that he wasn't any good at peeling or chopping and, besides, he said, she enjoyed all that stuff and was so good at it – he'd only ruin the dinner if he got involved! Also, he was planning on going for a twenty-mile ride with his cycling group in the afternoon, so he wouldn't have that much time to spare.

Arlie looked towards her husband, who was out in the garden shaking a box of cat biscuits and calling the cat's name into the darkness. It dawned on her that she hadn't seen the cat at all that day, which was particularly unusual, given the thing had a magnetic attraction to her father-in-law's lap.

"Not a clue where the fur-bag's got to," groused Marc, appearing at the kitchen door as Arlie stared at nothing in particular.

"I'm going to bed," she mumbled, and dragged herself upstairs. Later, Marc climbed into bed, kissed her on the neck and asked if everything was okay. She pretended to be asleep.

***

The next morning there was still no sign of the cat. This seemed to hugely upset Jake, a response Arlie found odd as her boy normally had little interest in the cat. But today, Jake was sporadically breaking into fits of crying, pounding his fists and asking where the cat was.

As Marc wandered in from in the garden, Jake pointed in the direction of the lounge and squeaked, "The tree!"

Marc bent over, ruffling his son's hair and kissing the bump on his forehead – which had thankfully gone down a fair amount overnight. "It wasn't the tree, Jakey. You just need to be more careful when you're running around. Right, Mum?"

Arlie didn't reply. She was gazing distractedly in the direction of the lounge.

"Arlie, you okay?" asked Marc, touching her gently on the shoulder. Arlie jolted with a fright, then shook her thoughts clear. "Yeah. Sorry. Nothing," she stammered.

***

The disappearance of the cat seemed to have disturbed Jake so greatly that he refused to even get onstage during the nativity later that day. Screaming and crying hysterically as the nursery teachers tried in vain to get his costume on, Arlie had to eventually take her son to the back of the church hall and watch as the rest of the children performed, with the occasional heads of the other parents turning her way, their looks of concern or judgement feeling like knives flung across the room. She just wanted to sleep.

Jake wasn't much better when she got him home. Her attempts to start on Christmas dinner prep were constantly derailed by Jake's bawling and crying. What she was hoping would be a couple of hours of peeling and chopping took her until late in the evening.

Arlie took a break to finally put Jake to bed and had begun to make tomorrow's dessert – a sherry-drenched variation of Christmas pudding – when in walked Marc, furrowing his brow at a messy kitchen full of half-finished vegetables.

He was clad head-to-toe in sweaty Lycra and wore those expensive cycling shoes that hook onto the pedals and make an infuriating clicking noise when walking.

"Did you get all of the presents?" he asked, still staring at the food.

Arlie's mouth dropped open. "What?!" she snapped. Marc recoiled as though touching a hot stove.

"Are you … Are you actually fucking *kidding* me?" she spluttered. "You've been out all day, riding your wanker bike with your wanker mates. Doing nothing to help me today." She could feel her face turn red as she grew ever more animated. "Did you know Jake's been a total … a total *shit* all day? He was so worked up over the cat, I had to take him home from nursery. He's been on my case all night, so I've barely got any of this done." She waved her arms at the table of vegetables. "And you're asking me about fucking *presents*?"

Marc stammered, a few vowels, nothing else. He looked like a fish gasping for air. "I'm sorry," he eventually managed to say. "I didn't realise you were under so much stress. You … you should have said."

Arlie exploded. "I shouldn't have to say! I shouldn't have to say, Marc! It's not the fucking Fifties. I'm not your stupid little housewife, no matter how much you or your parents want me to be! Jesus Christ!"

"I'm sorry, Arlie. I'm really sorry, you're right, I've been shit. I'm sorry," he bumbled, placing a Lycra-gloved hand on her shoulder.

"Of course I got all the presents, of course I did. I've done everything, all of it."

"I know," Marc said meekly. "I'm sorry. I only asked because I was just looking at the tree …" Arlie cocked her head and narrowed her eyes at him as he continued, "And it looked like there were a lot fewer than we – sorry, *you* – bought."

"What?" Arlie stared at her husband, her eyes widening. He started to reply but she marched out of the kitchen, into the lounge. Dropping to her knees in front of the tree she grabbed frantically at the presents around its base.

"Love, careful," said Marc. "You're ripping some of the paper."

But Arlie ignored him. He was right. There were at least half a dozen boxes missing – yet she'd put them there only this morning.

Suddenly, she froze. She sat up onto her haunches, staring at what she'd just picked up.

A collar. The cat's collar.

"What's that doing th—" began Marc, but Arlie grabbed his arm and dragged him out of the room as she backed away.

She had turned a ghostly white, her eyes bulging out of her head in terror. "It's the tree."

"What?" blustered Marc.

"It's the tree, Marc." She held up the cat's collar to his face. "It took the tinsel. It took your mum's scarf. Those presents. It took the cat." She gasped. "It tried to take Jacob!"

Marc placed a hand on each of her shoulders. "Arlie, you're not feeling right. It's the stress, it's gotten to you."

"No, Marc, you're not listening, it's—"

"You're right, Arlie, you're right. I've not been listening. And I'm sorry. I've let you take on too much of this Christmas and you weren't ready for it. My mum was right, we should have them over tomorrow. They can take care of all of this. You can—"

Arlie pushed his hands off her shoulders and backed towards the door. "Marc, you're not listening to me," she stuttered, before pointing to the lounge. "It's the tree. There's something not right about it. I knew it the day you brought it in."

Marc moved forward and tried to put his hands on her again, but she threw them off.

"I'm getting the fuck out of here," she said, holding her brow. "I need to get out of here. I need to think." She turned to Marc, walked closer to him. "Listen to me. When I get back either the tree's gone, or you are."

And with that, she grabbed her car keys and ran out of the house.

＊＊＊

Arlie drove for hours, circling the countryside around their house.

It was past midnight and the roads were empty but for taxis ferrying Christmas revellers to or from their festivities. She let the low hum of the engine calm her, following the curves of the roads this way and that as she tried to process the things she had seen over the preceding days. The branches of the tree, waving at her. Things going missing. The cat. Was this really happening?

This was insane. She had to accept it. Maybe Marc was right. Maybe his family were right, that she wasn't well, that she wasn't able to deal with the stress. Maybe she was just overreacting to all of this. Of course she was. She was blaming a few misplaced items on an evil tree. The cat would come back, it was prone to taking off for a few days at a time. It'd just slipped its collar during a play session beneath the tree. She was being insane. She needed to get home and apologise to Marc before she ruined Christmas any further.

＊＊＊

Opening the front door, Arlie was greeted by the sight of the old bedsheets laid out across the hallway. She felt a pang of guilt knowing that Marc had gone through with it and gotten rid of the tree. How to explain this to Jake tomorrow, she wondered.

As pleased as she was that Marc had taken her seriously enough to get rid of the tree, she suspected he had done so with some anger, since there were pine needles spread all over the hallway.

She could even see some as far as the entrance to the kitchen. A few steps more took her to the doorway of the lounge.

The lounge floor was covered in the bedsheets, all of which were dotted with pine needles. The mess was ten times that of when the tree was first brought in, with pine needles this time spread out across the entire room – even seemingly scattered across the furniture. Arlie's gazed was drawn to the corner of the room, and her throat suddenly turned dry.

The tree was still in its place.

And its branches were slowly, silently moving, back and forth, back and forth.

"Mummy," said Jake, who had padded into the room after her. "Why was Daddy shouting earlier?"

Arlie cried out and pulled her son close. At the base of the tree, she spotted a shoe. One of Marc's cycling shoes. And beyond it, lay the broken shards of the plastic base which had once housed the tree's trunk, now splintered in all directions.

A rustling, bristling noise began to emanate from the tree as its branches waved back and forth with increasing menace. It began to shudder and shake, trembling violently and spasming in every direction. Its branches appeared to be growing longer and they quickly twisted and spiralled outwards like tendrils, the crack of bark splintering as they expanded and reached out towards Arlie and her child.

She screamed as a branch whipped out, wrapping itself around her leg.

Jake screeched in panic as his mother was dragged across the floor towards this twitching, twisting, convulsing mass of branch and root. Arlie grabbed hold of the nearest support she could: the stone base of the fireplace.

The fire was still lit and she felt its oppressive heat on her skin as she held on.

She gripped with all her strength, the muscles in her shoulders pulsing in agony as she fought the strength of the roots pulling at her leg.

—

With one final, desperate burst of energy, Arlie stretched upwards, towards the fireplace and reached into it. Ignoring the searing pain on her hand, she grabbed the largest log – a brick-sized chunk of wood enveloped in flame – and, with her last ounce of strength, hurled it into the centre of the tree.

The Christmas tree seemed to almost wince, releasing her leg and letting out a low, creaking murmur as though crying out in pain. Arlie didn't hesitate. She jumped to her feet, grabbed her son and hauled him out of the room. The creaking, crackling, howling mass of fire and wood lurched after them, following them into the hallway and then the kitchen. Flames flickered up the walls of the house, spitting out embers and sparks as the splintering wood cracked and exploded under the heat.

But still, it pursued them.

As they made it into the kitchen, Arlie spotted the bottle of sherry still on the kitchen table. She grabbed it and turned to find the flaming, screeching tree towering above them both. She threw the bottle hard at its trunk, shattering it. Flaming liquid billowed upwards, engulfing the rest of the tree in fire. It let out a long, agonised moan, giving Arlie enough time to grab Jake and sprint into the garden. This time the tree did not follow.

***

Staring at her house as it burned in the crisp winter's night, Arlie was momentarily transfixed by the flames as they twisted and flickered, devouring the remnants of her home. Bathed in the orange glow and the warmth of the fire, she hugged her son.

Something soft touched her leg and she looked down to see the family cat, purring softly as it rubbed against her.

She smiled and looked back towards the house. She was enjoying a rare moment of tranquillity.

Black Ice

Kelly Creighton

At hometime, through the crumbling frame of her broken windscreen, Noelle stared back at the Other Mums standing by the school gates. They had to be foundered, standing nude-ankled like that in the snow. All sockless in mock croc skin pumps, their jeggings worming up their legs.

Here even the mums wore uniforms. In springtime it had been Nautical Tops. They'd dismounted their jeeps like a crew of sailors abandoning ship. Had the Other Mums never read magazines and therefore missed warnings against horizontal stripes? These warnings were the only thing Noelle remembered about magazines. But maybe the Other Mums were renegades too, in their own obedient ways.

Noelle's mum costume was seasonless: old tracksuits she'd kept and renamed Lounge Wear; a 24-hour clothing range, biker boots pulled on over the top. You had to love mornings, when you could drop the kids off at the kerb and stay snug at the wheel in your fleecy dressing gown.

In the afternoons Noelle had to get out of the car and join the Other Mums. Thankfully now they knew to keep away and had ceased asking her to join the PTA after what happened last time.

They'd only offered her the position of Treasurer to show that even if she judged books by covers, they Did Not. All that money in her care. Didn't Jonny only go and trouser it? After a week of questions, Noelle had to contact that Wee Woman in Donaghadee who gave loans. But one Other Mum was undeterred. She invited Noelle and the kids to her home that she'd decorated like a hotel. She'd wanted to show Noelle The Good Life so Noelle would want it herself. Noelle did not. In the kitchen the Other Mum gave a Ted Talk on The Virtues of Speaking Softly to Children – 'They listen better to whispers' – but when she found her own child pouring beakers of juice without asking her help, the Other Mum screamed till her face almost cracked. Noelle had never seen more hypocrisy in her life.

Her daughter Smudge took over care of the beakers, unfazed at the screaming, much used to it, unfortunately.

'I swear,' Noelle told Smudge, in mum solidarity, 'spill that and I'll kill you Stone Dead.'

'Oh, dear, it's just Mi Wadi,' said the Other Mum. 'We don't require actual threats on people's lives.'

'I'm not really going to kill her,' said Noelle. 'It's called a Figure of Speech.'

This Other Mum worked on obtaining a reciprocal invite which Noelle had no intention of issuing. She was Out. What would they say if they saw Noelle's place! The state of her back garden for one; the bottles of drink sitting out, for handiness.

They'd have had her an alcoholic at the school gates. 'It all computes,' they'd be saying, even though their homes had alcohol and more of it, but theirs was hidden away in bespoke bar areas safely away from children.

———

Pretty Storage made all the difference.

After another attempt to sweep the broken glass away Noelle got out of the car. Aware of the stares she joined the Other Mums without exactly joining. Out flew the kids with Christmas hats on and headbands with pom-poms, LED lights flickering and genuflecting, school bags fattened with jumpers, coats tied back-to-front-apron-style around their waists.

'Why is your coat off?' Other Mums said, real annoyed but acting faux-annoyed. 'Oh, I give up!'

Noelle had Given Up. She toyed with the idea of sending her kids in the next day in summer dress and shorts. This would be her Ted Talk: How to Build Your Child's Character. Kids raised like hers needed no one's approval. They were Survivors. And she'd send them in in summer uniform too, not least to piss the teachers off.

They'd Given Up too, at last. Thankfully, the last one had: the Awk-I-Mesh-With-Anyone One who thought she could sweeten Noelle, feeling all Anything is Possible since she'd lost the weight and taken to wearing Lycra – the apparent uniform of Recently Skinnies – as she ran around handing out leaflets for Slimming World.

Noelle loathed her most. She was no one's upcycling project.

Handsome came running and hugged her around the hips.

'Alright Handsome,' said Noelle. She'd always called him that because it wasn't his fault he wasn't. 'Right, Smudge.'

The girl's face was a pleasure but always grubby. She handed Noelle her school-bag to carry.

'What happened?' asked Smudge getting near to the car and seeing its every window broken. Soon aware of the slowing queue of rubbernecks, her face pinked.

Glass spilled out when Noelle opened the back door. It was ferocious. 'In youse pop,' she said.

'Is everything alright here?' asked an Other Mum, her eyes dark and clinquant.

'Everything's the best, and yourself?' Noelle said.

'Do you need me to call the police? What will I say happened?'

The Other Mum's boy ran ahead and tried to open her jeep setting off the alarm.

'Someone's stealing your car! Do you need me to call the police?' Noelle took out her phone.

Did the Other Mum think Noelle had no phone? She had a phone alright. Never credit, but she could take incoming calls. The Other Mum hurried up the lane, bleeping her bleepy thing.

'Wow,' said Handsome peering into the backseats. 'What is This?'

'Are you looking at my crystals?'

'It's broken glass,' said Smudge.

'Nah,' Noelle said, 'crystals. I'm going to sell them like Jack did.'

'Jack?'

'From that panto school took you to see. Remember how he got beans for his cow?'

'They were magic.'

'Well, so are those crystals.' She used the manufacturer's handbook to sweep more curds onto the ground.

'What really happened, Mum?' asked Smudge.

88

'I robbed a jewellery shop for Christmas money, drove into the shop window.'

'No you didn't.'

'Where are our windows gone, Mummy?' asked Handsome.

She thought for a minute. 'Remember your friend's daddy took you for a drive in that car with no roof.'

'Yeah.'

'You liked that, didn't you, wind in your face?'

'Uh-huh.'

'Well, I thought, I want a convertible too.'

Smudge shivered. Noelle was freezing now too, she'd felt the cold alright driving out of Belfast towards Newtownards, it was The Shock, then she grew hot with rabid fury, then calmer.

You have to be calm for the kids. Don't you?

'Who in the name of God,' her brother said when he saw the car. 'Was it Jonny?'

'Maybe … Indirectly.'

'What does that mean?'

'A friend of his, Not a Friend, someone Jonny pissed off saw my car outside Auntie's.'

'Shit. Where are you going to get the money to fix it?'

'I have a Wee Woman in Donaghadee I can ask.'

He sighed. 'Any sign of Jonny?'

'No, and sure didn't I want him gone?'

'Happy For You and all that, but he still has a duty to the kids. Look, I'll take this to my mate, get his best price for you.'

'Thank you.'

'Does that woman in Donaghadee ask a lot of interest?'

'Less than a pay-day loan.'

'You'll be paying for her off forever.'

'I've no other choice.'

'Bloody Jonny.'

***

The next day Child Benefit went in. Noelle got credit on her phone and took a bus to the shops. Christmas songs played, all the sad ones, songs Handsome called Lonely. Songs that managed to Resurrect the Dead.

Crossbars of zimmer frames clogged each aisle. Everyone needed and needed now The Thing behind her trolley. Everywhere she stood someone got in her way, in badness, it seemed. It was hard not to Lose One's Shit.

It was true, people went mad at Christmas. When she'd worked here she hated working Christmas.

People wanted serving quicker than normal, notwithstanding the longer queues, they'd snatched receipts out of her hand and rudely walked away.

'No, thank you,' Noelle had shouted after them, only a smidge of aggression in her passive aggressiveness. 'No, you have a Happy Christmas.'

That always got a Guilty Glance Back, if you kept your voice upbeat enough.

Aggression had lost all shades of subtly these days, it was now Post Box Red and spitting feathers. Noelle would never be that rude customer, she'd promised herself, who forgot that cashiers were humans too. She would say Hello and thank them, ask about their day.

That was the plan. Noelle forgot it.

In the queue the cashier chatted to the pregnant woman in front as Noelle Tetris-ed the toys and glanced up periodically. The conversation went on after the transaction was done. Noelle sighed loudly, not meaning to. Not able to hold it down.

'I don't know that woman,' said the cashier, feeling she must explain. 'She was telling me she's having baby number six.'

'Mad Bitch,' muttered Noelle.

'Two was enough for me.'

'Too much for me,' Noelle said, complaining But Not Really complaining.

Her two were the best mistakes she'd ever made. Where would she be without them?

The cashier scanned the toys and slipped into a trance. Someone behind was right up against Noelle, a hip and upper arm pushing against her.

She turned to look, expecting someone who Knew No Better but finding an older woman, designer glasses, fancy clutch bag in her hand, the woman's husband Tetris-ing wine bottles on the belt.

Noelle leaned back, she would not be pushed like this, and she was being pushed. She turned again and came nose to nose with a Real Bad Bitch. Noelle faced away again and stepped backwards, making sure she stood on toes.

'Sorry, I didn't know you were so close – didn't hurt you, did I?'

The woman stared back, recognising a Real Bad Bitch before her, too. Her husband stepped in, incognizant to subtle badness. 'Wild in here today, isn't it?' he said.

'Oh, it is,' said Noelle, 'same every year.'

'Only a week to go,' said the cashier, 'how did that creep up?'

'And yet they have Christmas on the same day every year,' the older woman deadpanned.

The cashier half-laughed. The woman behind pushed against Noelle again. Harder.

'Sorry,' Noelle said, because people from Ards say sorry but never when something is their fault, only when they are Wholly Not to Fault. 'Do you want past me?'

The older woman glared.

'Or do you want me to bend over and that way you can Crawl Up My Ass?'

The older woman stepped back while her husband stepped forward, opacity settling on his previously see-through face.

'So ... you must have a wee boy and wee girl,' said the cashier, trying to be friendlier; a Bomb Disposal Technician, like Noelle herself had once been.

'That's not on. I'm going to say something,' the man said.

'Leave it,' said the woman through gritted teeth.

Oh, those teeth, Noelle knew them well. Those teeth had given her pains in the jaw, down the neck, pains that spread upward. They'd evaded Brain Scans those pains.

'There is no bleeding.'

No bleed, no tumour, no swelling of any sort. The All Clear, they called it. Just a Plain Brain Noelle had. Then she woke one night with a toothache and could not get back over, that was unusual.

Even last night, after The Day She Had in Belfast, Noelle slept like a log. After the night of toothache Noelle went to the dentist despite avoiding her for years after cultivating An Irrational Fear.

'Your teeth are fine,' said the dentist, 'what you've done is pulled a muscle.'

'Pulled a muscle?'

'In your mouth.'

'Christ,' said Noelle. She wouldn't tell anyone that; it sounded like an occupational hazard for porn stars.

The dentist said, 'Copy me. Do This.' And moved her jaw left. 'Do That.' And moved it right. 'Do This.' Opened her mouth wide. 'And That.' She closed her mouth. 'But Don't Clench Your Teeth.'

Noelle did her workout and the headaches left, along with the toothache. Now she saw her whole face as a ball of elastic bands.

The cashier was telling her a story about her children, 'Children! They're grown up now ...' Noelle tried to listen, she moved her jaw from side to side, wide open and closed and looked outside at the snow-swollen sky.

'Think we're due a fresh dose,' said the cashier. 'Nice to see it. Last year was too mild, it Didn't Feel Like Christmas at all.'

The woman behind Noelle was still angering her. Was their showdown over?

What was it Jonny learned in that one Anger Management class he bobbed up for, before ducking out, being Not a Group Person. Yes, this was it:

'Ask yourself,' he'd scoffed, 'if this will matter in a week's time.'

——

Would this older woman behind Noelle matter in a week? No. Of course not. By then these toys she was trolleying would be unpackaged, part of the furniture.

The cashier trilled along to Shakin' Stevens. She looked happy, she was Good at Faking It. She had tinsel in her hair, Noelle noticed now, as she took her payment, had Noelle swipe her loyalty card and looked right at her, for the first time. There was a flash of distress in the cashier's eyes like a hostage would have, it made Noelle Feel Like Shit. Like Jonny. Only he never cared enough to Feel Like the Shit he was.

Noelle had a dark compost of thoughts then: starting with Smudge creeping down the stairs and not seeing Mummy Kissing Santa Claus but seeing Daddy Throwing Whatever Came Handy at Mummy's Head or working himself up to. And the rest. Things children shouldn't see.

Handsome always seemed to sleep through, but how could you be sure? And soon he'd be bigger, more easily woken. It would do a boy no good to see his father act in such a way.

Next thought:

'What is that round your eye?' Handsome said, the morning after one such night.

'I'm a panda today,' Noelle told him. She remembered this now, wheeling the trolley out into the snow.

'Then I want to be a panda.'

'No you don't. Pandas eat leaves, they can't have sweets.' He'd been about to blub. 'Fine, come here.' Noelle painted around Handsome's eye black and dropped him off at school.

In the afternoon the teacher came out of the gate and said, 'Afraid we have a policy about no make-up.'

'Can I see it?' asked Noelle.

'You may not, because it's not a Written Policy. We simply can't allow make-up for one and Not the Rest.'

This teacher, like Many Teachers, talked to everyone, adults too, like children. Noelle loathed that. She took off her sunglasses, reached into her bag, found Smudge's wet wipes and wiped the correction pen from her left eye. 'Better?' she asked with the shiner exposed.

'Look at Mummy,' said Handsome, 'we are both Pandas today.'

What bloody great kids I have, Noelle thought hauling their toys into the boot of the taxi and onto the back seats. The driver sat watching her from all angles, keeping himself warm, the meter already started.

They didn't say a word on the way home. The Pogues played, then The Waitresses, then Mud. She lugged Every Last Box out onto her empty-bar-snow driveway and posted a tenner through his down-a-crack window.

'No, happy Christmas to you,' she shouted as he took off with a skid.

Noelle went round the back to the shed, head down, never looking at that mess of a garden, ignoring it she got the ladder and brought it into the house and up the stairs, then Noelle hauled the toys indoors.

Trembling on the ladder – Jonny's Old Job – she shoved the bags up into the square mouth above her head. Clammily she poured herself a beer after a job well done, then another, since she'd been relieved of driving duties.

She hid the ladder and walked to school, warmer slightly, revived by drink.

As she walked Noelle thought about the Nice Scared Cashier. Noelle wondered if she had the patience to work there again. She'd done it before but she'd changed; she had no space for being serviceable anymore. Probably wouldn't last a day in that place.

Crabbit she stood at the school gates. The Other Mums were in situ, gossiping. They all had their hair up. That was no good, Noelle theorised. Hair Up meant no sex that night.

And another thing Noelle noticed, if The Husbands ever came to school, say, if it was A Special Day, school play or that kind of thing, the Other Mums' hair would be down, they would be hair-tossing in front of The Husbands. The Husbands didn't seem to notice. They did This School Thing so rarely they blundered about, trying to smile and chat to Other People, even Noelle. Huge mistake.

They didn't know Proper Etiquette about talking only to people who were dressed in the same uniform as their own wives. Avoid Mums in slept-in tracksuits, at all costs.

The Husbands were there to talk to their wife, to Look Lovingly at Her, for the Other Mums to see this breathing moving Instagram. The Husbands would get sex that night for their effort. It was a theory Noelle was proud of.

Only one Husband came to the school gates regularly.

Correction: the bench facing it. (Technically an Ex Husband.) He always sat on his bench, looking destructive. The Other Mums pretended he wasn't there. His Ex Wife never did the school runs anymore. But one day, Noelle got there early and nabbed the prime spot so she wouldn't have to leave the car and could stay in her dressing gown, and saw the Ex Wife with a New Fella.

Noelle watched them walk down the lane, then back in front of the school. No one else was about yet. The Other Mums would have loved to see the sunglasses the Ex Wife was wearing: red-framed, heart-shaped. She was holding this New Fella's hand and with her free hand tried to pull a leaf from a tree and ended up breaking the whole branch off. But She Held On and brought it into the car and waited there for her kids.

Now Noelle stood at the gate and half-listened to the Festive Shit-Chat about Centrepieces for the Table and Garlands for the Fireplace. How the Other Mums's floral-display frivolity bored her!

'They've got debt up to their eyeballs, too,' said Jonny once, 'don't be fooled.'

True, they were mums like her, Stay At Homes, but one thing they had that she didn't, was a man. If that made much difference! Jonny's painting-decorating money was always his. And he'd wanted her at home, immured. How would Noelle get a job now anyway with a seven-year hole in her CV?

'Volunteer somewhere, would you not,' Auntie had been saying when Noelle saw that fucker out the front, eyeing the car up. Noelle was visiting with a tin of petticoat tails and a pretty snow-scene Christmas card, quietly cursing the petrol money to Belfast. But she was glad she was free again to see the people Jonny hadn't liked her seeing. Which was everyone, really.

'Volunteer,' said Auntie, 'then someone will give you a reference …'

'A reference,' she tutted, seeing him go, turning back to Auntie. 'I never thought about references.'

'That's why I'm saying, if you volunteer …'

Next he was back, smashing up her wee car.

'What in the name of God in heaven!' Auntie jumped up. He was Going At It with a steering wheel lock, swinging it back, about to do the second window. Noelle bolted outside.

'You Jonny's wife?' he asked. 'Tell him hello.'

She went to run and nearly slipped on black ice. Auntie screamed as the windows exploded inwards. He walked to the other side of the car.

'Stop it!' Noelle screamed. 'Jonny's Gone!'

Next he did the windscreen. 'Call it even,' he said.

She didn't know what this was over but nothing surprised her, Jonny befriended unsavoury types and quickly they unfriended him.

'Car's in getting fixed today,' she said as the kids came out of the school gate.

They were not happy to walk. The snow had lost its oddity for the kids. At least, she thought, they had coats and gloves, and a roof over their heads and toys under that roof. Just as well, because Noelle had nothing left to give away. She'd eBayed old toys, baby stuff, her wedding dress, wedding ring.

It wouldn't matter who came to her door Looking For Jonny, her kids would not go without and that's all there was to it.

She gave Handsome a piggy back home, still not used to being in school till two, his eyes were full of zeds, while Smudge stomped ahead, splenetic.

Noelle moved her jaw left and right, opened her mouth wide and closed it.

'Tired, Mummy?' asked Handsome thinking she was yawning.

'Nope,' she said, 'I slept Like A Log last night.'

***

The next day was a two-hour school day, to watch Elf and eat Haribo. Still without wheels she tried to get the time in at the local Garden Centre.

To call it a Garden Centre was indeed a cheek, there was a tiny outdoor planty area and indoors, rails of clothes for elderly ladies.

Noelle listened to Bing Crosby, Pretenders, East 17, Elton John, and various artists, fondled tree baubles and checked the prices over and over, hoping they'd change. She shunned twelve offers of help by cashiers in the festive spirit, having a Right Old Laugh together. Noelle plucked up the courage to ask if they were looking for staff.

'Not at this time of year,' she was told, 'we have seasonals, and then it'll go quiet again. If we are, there will be a sign in the window. Keep an eye out.'

She heard the Other Mums coming downstairs, saw those bare ankles, the crocodile stampede. They'd been in the first floor cafe supping cinnamon-spiced skinny lattes, splitting a mince pie seven ways, no doubt.

'I'll keep an eye out,' Noelle said and escaped outside where she stared at the plants.

The automatic doors opened and in came kids with the same uniform as Handsome and Smudge. These kids were older. The school choir, they lined up beside the plants.

The Other Mums followed suit with iPads and a glass of mulled wine produced by Garden Centre staff. Noelle sidled over, took a cup and watched the poor half-frozen kids as they sang Silent Night looking ill, infectious and mortified.

Her phone buzzed. Her brother, texting that her car was ready.

Whats ur excess?

On my insurance like

Yes, u do have insurance?

It was the first thing to go, first before life insurance, first before home, building and contents. She went outside-outside and phoned him. 'I'll just lift the full whack.'

'Don't tell me you don't have insurance, Noelle.'

'You didn't mention it the other day.'

'Insurance is Not A New Thing. What if you'da had an accident and it was your fault?'

'No more questions at this stage, your honour,' Noelle said and hung up, not in the mood to be lectured, never in the mood For That.

Noelle called the Wee Woman in Donaghadee and told her the sums. The Wee Woman told her to drive over and collect but Noelle explained she wouldn't have a car until after she had the dough and asked if they could arrange something via PayPal, afraid, because cash Went Like Water through her fingers. But the Wee Woman didn't work like that.

'Can you bring me to Donaghadee first, love?' she asked her brother when he pulled up in his car outside the school.

'You are joking!' he said. He high-fived the kids as they climbed in the back and buckled up.

'Listen,' said Noelle, 'that Wee Woman has mountains of cash in the house. Someone desperate could take advantage.'

'I'm seeing a different side to you lately, lady.'

'How?'

'You sound like you want to take advantage of her. You're getting on like you want to Kill Her and Take Her Money.'

'Mummy doesn't Kill People,' said Smudge, 'it's just a figure of speech.'

He sighed. 'Right, right, I have a bit of wedge on a credit card since I paid my car off.'

'No, no.'

'I insist. Don't even give it back. I've no need for it.'

'Yes you do.'

'Aye, but you're about to do something mad. You have a deranged look in your eye lately, it's since Jonny left.'

'It's just this time of year. Christmas sends people loop-de-loop.'

'It does right enough, but they'll Not Do Without, them two, and that's not what Christmas is about any road.'

'What is it about?'

'The baby Jesus,' shouted Handsome.

'And family,' said Smudge, 'and love.'

'Look,' said her brother, pulling into the garage, 'your wee car's as good as new. Or, good as it was.'

'Can we keep the jewels?' asked Handsome.

'What jewels?'

'Mummy robbed a jewellery shop for gems. That's what was on the floor and the seats.'

'True,' said Noelle. 'Can't lie.'

'You want to watch what you say, he'll go and tell his teacher.'

'He won't.'

'Believe me, Noelle, be careful. The things I've been pulled up on that my kids have made up or I've told them as a joke. Wouldn't take you to be a body with a skeleton.'

At home Elf was on the TV. Handsome was happy to watch it again.

In the kitchen Smudge hung about Noelle. 'Mum,' she said, 'after Christmas can I have my room painted pink?'

'You hate pink.'

'No, I hate yellow.'

'You just had it done yellow in November.'

'Can you paint it pink next?'

A bowl of shells still sat by the sink, years on. Smudge had always lifted the spoils of the beach when she was little and said, 'For you, Mummy.' Noelle understood these as priceless gifts. Maybe Smudge would understand.

'Love, Daddy's Away and I have no job, that pays ... I can't do everything. I'd like to but I just can't afford to. I'd get into trouble trying.'

'I won't get you into trouble.'

'I know that. You wouldn't mean to. And Daddy leaving, you know that isn't your fault either.'

'It's yours.'

Noelle felt a jag in the heart. 'No, it's his. Look, we were just fighting a lot.'

'But you ...' Smudge made a fist and held up her thumb, then ran the thumb along her throat and made a squelch sound. 'You, did That to Dad.' Noelle felt sick.

'It's okay. I haven't told my bestie,' said Smudge, 'and we tell each other Secrets. But I know this is Family Secret.'

'I don't know what you mean, Smudge. Out of the way, I need to start dinner.' Noelle pulled the chicken nuggets bag from the freezer, her head aching.

'Isn't daddy dead?'

'Shush! What do you think you heard?' Noelle whispered.

'You saying, I'll kill you Stone Dead.'

'No, he said that to me. Always saying that to me, so he was.'

'It was you. I thought it was the Christmas tree you were pulling through the garden but I saw the shoes. Behind the shed the next day, I felt.'

'What?'

'Laces and ... socks. There was no Christmas tree up.'

'Awk, that's been a dream!'

'It wasn't. I touched him with this hand.' She waved a hand in Noelle's face, Noelle caught her wrist then gently released it.

'You know what I love most about you, Smudge, your brilliant imagination.'

'Thank you, Mummy,' Smudge said smiling.

After tea Noelle texted her brother: *One Last Favour?* She told him she had a date.

Where'd u find time 2 meet some1 new?

There were the people who made the mess and the people who always cleaned it up. Right now her brother thought he was the one cleaning up. But really, it had always been Noelle.

'Time you had a bit of fun,' said her sister-in-law at the door as the kids ran off to find their cousins.

'You two go out on Old Year's Night,' said Noelle, 'I'll repay the sleepover.'

She imagined Smudge's pillow-talk with her girl cousins. 'Wanna hear a Family Secret?'

Oh, Christ!

At home Noelle kicked off her high heels, pulled her dress off and Jonny's overalls on. Behind the shed she knelt in the snow and watched for neighbours' lights going on or blinds flickering. No signs of a pulse.

She dug away stones and soil, and quickly found his shoe. Then, down a bit deeper, the other. Unearthed him bit by bit, cocooned in an old duvet cover. She heaved him out, had parked the car as far up the drive as she could.

'Just a single mum moving presents around,' she planned to say to neighbours who never materialised because no one was home, they were at parties, or on real dates. Maybe that would be her in Future Years, came the gust of a thought, while she wheelbarrowed his rigid body to the back of the car where the seats were pushed down flat.

Noelle sat in the front, sweating. She wound down the window to let his rancid smell out. The air was static, cold and still. As she drove it began to snow and the town went silent. The tyre tracks were soon covered with snow. She couldn't deny how pretty everything seemed, looking outward. A Pretty Pollution.

Down by the lough there was snow on the sand. It looked just like the Christmas card she gave her aunt.

Holiday Greetings from Newtownards.

Angel's Breath

Jo Zebedee

Winter was Mum's favourite time of the year. I can imagine her now, as if she were alive, in her red bobble hat and thick scarf. She loved the crisp days and sharp frosts. When there was snow in the forecast, she'd sit by the window, blinds open, to watch for it. She'd flit between weather forecasts until she found one that said heavy snow, and then she'd promise us drifts of six feet when all we got was sleet.

From the first appearance of Orion in the sky, the Winter Hunter, to the dark days of January, my mother came alive. Until last year.

Last year my mother died. On her last night in the hospice room the rain that had been splashing the windows stopped and a cold descended so that the path outside sparkled in the darkness.

She wouldn't let us draw the curtains, just as she never had on winter nights.

An hour later, from nowhere — at least not on any forecast any of us knew of — the snow arrived. Real snow. Thick, from the arctic, the type that sticks.

It fell heavier and heavier, covering the path and shrouding the bushes, until we were held in the room. It felt like the window was the glass of a snow globe and that we were just figures to be shook up, our lives crashing around us.

It was Mark who bent over and whispered for Mum to look outside. She'd always open her eyes for him. Her golden son, smart and funny. She adored him, and me, and we always knew it. Her heavy eyes opened and she saw the snow and smiled. She was still smiling when she died.

Grief ripped me. I put up no lights that Christmas — although Dad did try. He drew the line at the reindeer in the garden, though: said he'd always hated the evil-looking git. I barely got out of bed on the day itself, and only did so because Noreen wanted me to go to her house for the meal. That's my daughter, taking care of me. She claimed it'd break up the day, and save her dragging Abby and the baby out, but I knew the real reason.

We'd never had Christmas in her house before.

I doubted she'd even know what to do with a turkey but I still said yes because we hoped it wouldn't be like in my house, where I'd be seeing my mother of Christmas pasts in every corner.

Except, of course, I still saw her. Reading the cracker jokes loudly. Making us put on our hats for the pictures. Pictures upon pictures upon pictures, my lifetime stretching in a series of cracker hats. Noreen didn't have crackers on the table. She knew none of us would be able to look at a hat, let alone wear one, just as we all knew the jokes were never really funny.

I still saw Mum through January, past her birthday in February and into March. Quick glances of someone ahead of me on the path, who I was sure was her. The red bobble hat on the dog-walker, the exact shade of red, the same jaunty step. Her voice, singing along to Queen, asking not to stop now.

On Mother's Day I cried like I was a child again and there was no one to hold me, shush me, tell me things would be fine.

It was Mark who tried to pull me up. He came into my kitchen, one bright day, and took out one of the chairs. The tulips were drowsy on the windowsill, marking the end of winter.

"I have a new job," he announced, slightly smug.

He sat on the chair back to front, the way he always did. Said his legs were too long the other way. "Pour us a cuppa, Cathy, and I'll tell you about it."

That was how Mark coped: keeping busy, keeping connected, reminding me, and Dad, that life had to go on. It's what Mum would have wanted, he said, and he was right, I suppose. I managed to rouse myself and make the tea. My limbs felt heavy, as if I was moving underwater, but that was the new normal.

"So what's the job?" I asked, without much hope of understanding. Mark works in astrophysics. I can't tell you how pleased Mum was when that happened. She said it was all down to her, introducing him to the stars as a kid. Which doesn't explain why I've ended up as a corporate manager in the health service but hey-ho. Evidence does as evidence likes.

"I'm working on the Orion Nebula project." He took the cup from me and dunked five sugars in it, and I managed not to tell him – again – that it was impossible to taste more than three. "We're planning a probe launch later this year. It'll put Hubble to shame."

Little Abby wandered in, three years old and cheeky as could be. Tuesdays were my days for doing the childminding. Mostly, Tuesdays were what kept me going.

"What's an 'ebula?" she asked.

"Oh, you'll like it," said Mark as she clambered on his knee. She loved him, called him her uncle Mark even though he's technically the next generation up. He said he wasn't about to add Great to his name just yet. "It's a stellar nursery."

I had visions of nurses tucking stars into bed and singing them to sleep. He grinned at me, and I reckoned he knew exactly what I was thinking. I couldn't help smiling back.

"It's where stars are born, Abby. How cool is that?" He tapped the table, at me. "We going to capture a star being born. On camera, so that we can all see it, closer than anyone else has managed to."

"When?" I asked because, okay, a childhood of watching the stars made the idea of seeing one being born pretty cool. A prickle made my arm jerk and twitch, as if I was breaking free of the cocoon I'd been in.

"In about 100 years," he replied, deadpan. And then he asked me for Mum's lipsticks. When he explained why, I had to hunt one out of the box I'd taken, of her personals from the hospice, and give him it. And, inside, for the first time I felt a small flicker of something like excitement.

We decided to scatter Mum's ashes on a clear night, close to the anniversary of her death. Just the six of us: Dad, Mark and me, then Noreen and the two little ones.

"Let's do it at night," said Dad. "Under the stars."

"Perfect," said Mark and I together, and then I left it to Mark to work out the details. He was an astrophysicist after all. Plus, I realised for the first time – he, too, was more alive. When I'd been dead, not noticing things around me, he'd been cocooned too. I just hadn't been able to see it.

***

Wednesday morning, mid-December. This year I had managed to put up lights and decorations, even though my heart wasn't into it. Abby loved them, though, and Jolene, the baby, watched them with wide eyes.

The day was cold enough for a hard frost, so that the grass was white-tipped and the roof of the shed white. The phone rang before it was even eight o'clock and my heart thumped.

"When?" I asked, grabbing the handset. I didn't have to look at the number. Only a few people called me on the landline these days.

"Friday," said Mark. "It's perfect conditions. Clear, not too much wind. It'll be cold, but that's okay, isn't it?"

"Yeah." We used to stand for hours, in the cold, watching for shooting stars that streaked and were gone in seconds. Everyone else looked in August. They didn't realise the December shower, the Ursids, were better.

The excuse of cold was for wimps, not my mother's children. "I'll let Noreen know."

"Good. I'll take Dad. We can go in convoy." His voice was serious and that made me smile. It felt like we were undercover agents. I hung up and stared at the phone. I suppose we were, of sorts.

***

Noreen came for me at 10 pm on the dot. The baby was asleep in her car seat but little Abby wasn't. She was beyond excitement, jittering and talking about getting to stay up late and saying goodbye to Nana. When I saw her excitement, how she pointed out the stars in the sky as we drove along – she even knew the Plough – and chatted about the frosty road and how pretty it was, I knew my mother hadn't gone away, not really. Abby might not remember her – nor Jolene, the baby – but she'd know her. I'd see to it, in the stories I told.

I wondered if she would remember tonight and thought it likely that it would become her first memory; the night we let Nana go, under the stars and Orion, the hunter who'd watch over her as she left. I wondered how she'd remember me. As a ghost, still lost in grief, or as someone full of life. It made me wish I'd put on some lipstick and cheered myself up but I hadn't cared about that sort of thing in a year.

At the roundabout at the edge of town, Mark's car was parked up. He pulled out as we approached. We drove two junctions down, past the football stadium, and headed onto the moors.

The town before us was lit up, laced lights following the roads and estates. It fell away, until the lights were pinpricks, nothing more, and there was only our car, tyres swishing, and Mark's.

It felt clandestine, almost sneaky. And then there was only darkness and cat's-eyes on the road.

Mark took a left, off the road onto a track. Noreen cursed under her breath as we followed him over scree, up the hill, the engine protesting as she changed down a gear, and then another.

We pulled into a layby beside a stile. Noreen turned the car lights off. Mark appeared out of nowhere, a greyed out ghost, and lifted little Jolene from her seat.

She roused and he shushed her, holding her snug on his shoulder as we set off up the hill. He would have been a great dad, I thought as always, but said nothing.

There hadn't been the same chances to adopt when he'd been younger and now he claimed he and Samuel were too old, too set in their ways, to do it now. Instead, he'd keep being a great uncle. Without the capital G.

He stepped over the stile. Dad helped Abby over. She was quieter now, more serious. She placed her feet carefully and stepped down instead of jumping. She stopped and looked around the field, eyes wide. Yes, she would remember this night.

"Don't put on any torches, remember?" said Mark. He had Jolene tight against his shoulder. "Let your eyes adjust, Abby. We have time."

We stood, silent sentinels. I began to make out the line of the hedgerow. The field grew sharper, until I could see the tramline that led across it.

This was rambler territory, and the ground was hard with frost on the rudimentary path, and reasonably easy to pick our way across.

Mark led, then Dad and Abby, side by side. At the back, Noreen and I. We didn't talk. We didn't need to. More, we didn't want to.

We climbed under the magic of the night and stars, here on this exposed hilltop, in the middle of nowhere, and I'd never felt closer to my mother.

More than once, I looked back, sure I'd see her behind us, urging us to the peak and the best view.

It took forever, it felt like, but was really only half an hour until we reached the top. Then, we stood. Mark and I were veterans of this: we both wore gloves. Gently, he took something from his pocket and handed it to Abby, telling her to close her hands around it, and I knew it must be a hand-warmer, one that you snapped and it gave heat.

Dad stamped his feet, but didn't complain. He had never loved standing outside in the freezing cold, so Mum had inflicted it on us instead. Through the Perseids to spotting Jupiter, Venus and Mars in conjunction, meaning whatever she had read about it. We huddled together to keep warm. I pulled Abby close to me. Her body was sturdy and warm against my knee. I pointed out constellations, and told her stories about them. We were a family united again. Not separate pools of grief but together and strong.

"Grandma?" asked Abby. She pulled on my leg, the way she did when she wanted me to crouch down to her level and I did.

"What is it, love?" I asked.

"Where's Orion?"

Life went back 40 years to when I was a child, my own mother showing me. I pointed to the south-west.

"See the three brightest stars?" I said. "All in a row? Three of them?"

She nodded.

"That's his belt. And see the stars below? That's his sword. And that purple bit? It looks like a cloud."

"I do!" she said.

"That's where it's going to happen," I told her.

"When?"

In 2000 years, I could have told her, but she would never have understood. I looked up at Mark who juggled Jolene to look at his watch.

"Three minutes," he said, and we settled down to watch, crouched down at Abby's level. Dad threatened he might never get back up again. He brought his bag to the front of him – a plastic supermarket one, of all things; Dad is not sentimental – and lifted out Mum's casket. The kids had decorated it with star stickers that glowed in the dark. I had added three of them in a line.

"Orion," said Abby, touching them.

"Orion," I agreed.

"I'm ready," Dad said.

"And me," said Noreen.

I didn't think I would ever be ready to let her go, but Mark gave me a nudge and a half-wink, and I bucked myself up. This was the night we did her the honour she was due. The night we sent her up to the stars.

"Ready."

Dad held his finger up to the wind, to work out the direction of the wind. He stood up and prised off the lid of the casket.

I lifted Abby up — she wasn't so little anymore, but growing into a girl not a toddler, her arms and legs gangly, like a bird's.

"Ready for Nana Mary?" I said. She nodded. I would hold this night forever, the crisp winter air, the cleanness of it all around me. The perfect children, carrying our light into the future.

Dad lifted the casket, and the dust escaped in a puff of white. He shook it, to be sure everything had been released, and then set the casket back into its bag. It felt like an anticlimax, when I knew it was only an entrée.

"Any moment now," said Mark. "Watch. Coming across Sagittarius. Three – two – one…"

A flare of light streaked the sky, brighter than any shooting star. It travelled above us, faster and faster, going up into the sky and space beyond. It would travel for 100 years.

Dad stumbled back. "What's that?"

The glorious moment of a surprise held by me and Mark and no one else for months.

"That was the Orion probe," said Mark. "I've been working on finalising the broadcast package on it." His eyes watched the probe as it disappeared. "I added a little extra into the payload. Something just for us."

I stepped forwards, Amy still in my arms, as Mark opened Dad's hand and placed an empty lipstick casing into it.

"When the probe reaches the place where a star will be born," Mark said, "it will throw itself into the gases that will become the new star. It will photograph everything and then be sucked into the gases when they implode. It will become part of the star."

My father shivers. I think he understands what's coming now. I move against him, my strength to his. He's old, I realise. My mother will never be old.

"Her DNA is on the probe," I say. "We used her lipstick." Her bright, bright lipstick that no one could ignore. The bright lipstick that I haven't brought myself to wear. I'm not like her, not flashy and brave. I'm just solid me, reliable and boring.

"The DNA strand is held in the probe," said Mark. "I could have inserted its code into the data bank but I didn't want just that. I wanted more." He holds Jolene against him. He reaches over and brushes a wisp of hair back from Abby's forehead. "I sent a piece of the lipstick, instead. When the star is formed, Mum will be part of it. She'll live forever, in a way."

Dad's crying. I've never seen him cry, my unsentimental dad. Even at the funeral, he held himself apart from the mourners, together and unbroken.

Behind me, the wind stirred, like angel's breath on my neck. Like a silent thankyou from a ghost.

We walked back to the cars. It was harder going downhill. Abby was tired, and Mark gave Jolene to Noreen, and carried his other niece down, held against him, a precious treasure. We parted at the cars, him and dad in one, me and the girls in the other. While Noreen strapped the children in, I reached into my purse.

I lifted out the lipstick and opened it. In the car's interior light it was a slash of deep red, not as bright as in the day.

I turned the mirror down and brought the lipstick to my face. I hesitated. Waited for my eyes to stop burning, and my vision to clear. And then, firmly, sharply, I put the lipstick to my lips and painted it on. Blotted it, and painted it again. Made it bright, bright, shining bright. I faced myself in the mirror.

No more hiding. I only have one life, and it's for living.

As Noreen got into the car she glanced over at me, and grinned.

"Nice lipstick, Mum," she said. "It suits you."

And it did. We said no more because everything was done and the night was deep and starred and the magic had been cast. My mother would live forever, in Orion, her winter-hunter constellation.

Slay-Ride

Simon Maltman

1

The reindeer tore through the sky with such force, it appeared as if the Tower of London might crumble as they rushed past it. The reins were pulled tighter, his grip firm. An empty alley in Whitechapel was found to set down for a few minutes, so he could have a smoke of his pipe. St. Nicholas exhaled heavily, his breath already like smoke, wisping away from his dirty-white beard.

"Good boys," he said gruffly, placing a hand on Comet's back.

His thick, dark green coat was smeared with ash and soot. Its plump outline heaved in and out with every breath. The shadowy night was freezing and unforgiving. He reached inside the coat and rummaged for his pipe.

In one day it would be Christmas Day.

In a week and the year of 1889 would begin.

St. Nicholas would see neither.

The knife was already at his throat before old St. Nick knew anything of the attack. He hadn't time to react before the blade sliced through his neck and throat. He stood up, staggering, his hands grasping at his throat. The reindeer knew something was wrong; making guttural, keening sounds. The noises from St. Nicholas were no better.

His fingers couldn't stop the flow – immediately his stained coat was splattered with thick blood. Soon it would turn red. He fell over the side of the sleigh and out onto the hard cobblestones. He was dead before he hit the ground.

Jack wiped the blade on his long flowing black coat, then hid it back inside his breast pocket. He stood over his prey.

It was *him*.

That man with many names. Now he was dead.

He had several himself; *Leather Apron, The Whitechapel Murderer, Jack the Ripper.*

The alley was deathly quiet. He regarded the dead saint with his cold stare, then looked down at his clothes. Beneath his black coat was an old grey suit, with a butcher's apron on top of it. It was streaked with new blood and marbled with various shades from previous ventures. He scratched at his chin, then at the handlebar moustache. Checking over his shoulder, he pulled off his coat in a flurry and threw it to the wet ground. Then Jack heaved the body roughly back and forth until he had managed to pull off the thick green coat. He wrapped it around himself, swamping his lean shape within it.

The four reindeer turned to look at him; scornfully he thought. He leaned over the sleigh and pulled up the huge covering at the back. As he looked beneath it, his eyes danced inside his head. He pulled the cover back down, before climbing up onto the wooden seat. There the reins lay idle on the dusty and scored mahogany floor.

Tentatively he sat for a moment and held the long black leather between his knees. Then he stood, bracing himself. He raised the reins, and all at once whipped them down on the beasts, roaring, "Yaaah!" The reindeer responded instantly, galloping forwards along the alley. Faster, faster they went, as he wildly whipped the reins up and down.

"Come on, blast you!" he cried.

Then… up… up they climbed, higher… higher.

Jack let out a gasp as they inched over the top of a ragged tenement block.

"Haha!" he screamed, a freakish delight etched on his face.

2

They soared high over Westminster Palace. Though only a few decades old, the stone already seemed dulled, worn down by the wickedness of the city. Or at the very least now, coated in a layer of the city's dirt and filth. Around and round, they circled the city. Jack cackled at his most maniacal, as they swooped low over Tower Bridge, still only half-completed. The huge coat shielded him against the biting wind. Operating the sleigh felt strangely simple, natural. It was if there was a power emulating from the coat itself. He led his reindeer back towards Whitechapel. They set down on the roof of a red-bricked ruin of a place. It was somewhere he knew well. The team groaned and panted now back on solid ground again. Jack hopped out of the sleigh and carefully crossed the litter of broken tiles, constituting a roof. He stopped at the tall, crooked chimney pot. Even from up there the building reeked of desperation, grime, money and sex. He gingerly climbed into the chimney itself, unsure but eager. His urges had already overwhelmed him. Just as he slipped his other foot in, he felt a rush, a sweat, and the next he knew he was stood in the hearth below. Again, it felt as if the coat had supplied an invisible helping hand. Jack moved off immediately across the sparsely furnished candlelit room. He moved quickly and cautiously, unable to avoid all creaks from the ancient floor. Drunken laughter, strained bed springs and primal calls could be heard from other rooms.

He smiled and slid off along the hallway. Soon his knife was drawn and it went about its cruel and careful work. Door to door. Man and woman fell the same, the blade sliced open all flesh in its wake.

He had only killed women before. Again the coat brought him some unseen, additional strength, guiding him and leading him from room to room. By the end of the slaughter, the knife was more blood than steel. He wiped it over and over against the baggy tail of the coat. The smearing and splattering almost transforming it fully to red.

He visited two more brothels close by. The results were the same. This time he cackled as he went about his work. He howled as bodies, who minutes before were in the throws of primal passion, were now disembowelled and dismembered.

Then off he went, back into the sky, circling the city. He was its dark prince.

Then a thought struck him, "Why only remain in London?"

Wasn't there a whole world out there that he could now explore?

Jack dragged the reins and forced his unwilling team towards the sea. The sleigh rose up over Regent's Street. He could hear carol singers somewhere below and he grimaced. Before disappearing into the sky, a tavern below spilled out its last revellers. Oscar Wilde stumbled along the cobbles, sharing a bottle of wine with a male companion. He looked up at just the right moment to see the crazed Jack and sleigh, pulled by the weary reindeer streaking across the night sky.

He blinked repeatedly, declaring to himself, "The truth is rarely pure and never simple."

3

In but a few minutes, Jack was descending upon the sprawling, Baroque Palace of Schonbrunn. Resting on the roof of the seat of The Hapsburgs' Austrian empire, he prepared himself for his next kills. Allowing the reindeer time to catch their breath, he gazed over the city and dwelled on what delights it may offer him.

Then he was hovering above the enormous Versailles imitation again, flying over the huge gardens and its own private zoo. On to Vienna, on to feed his need.

Jack guided the reindeer across the city, passing both the five-hundred-year-old St. Stephen's Cathedral and the palace of Belvedere. He guided the team to descend down low by the banks of The Danube. The putrid odour of human excrement cutting through the cold reminded him of home. He landed on a shanty roof of a row of houses down by the docks. He was unlucky with the first home being empty. His knife yearned for more blood. The second house contained a family of five. The killing of them was enough to stave off the hunger. The third house was a brothel. There he greedily laid waste to everyone inside. That satisfied him, for now. Circling the city once more, his cackle could be heard echoing over the streets below. Blood dripped now from the saturated coat itself, staining the mahogany wood of the floor of the sleigh. His black heart pounded hard within his chest. The blood rushing around his body felt faster than normal. He was truly alive! His laughter stopped for long enough for him to wholly savour the moment.

This; surely the greatest night of his life.

Then there was a new sound seeping into the air. He pulled the team this way and that, searching out the noise. Music. A melancholic, but beautiful sonata swam out from the Vienna State Opera. Jack located the brand new opera house and landed the sleigh gently on to the immense roof. The beautifully performed music drifted purposefully through the roof and directly into the sleigh.

Johannes Brahms was inside conducting the orchestra himself, the musicians the finest Austria had to offer. It stunned Jack into stillness. The beautiful music haunted him. He closed his eyes. He sat there drifting for a few moments, as if on opiates.

He opened his eyes again and looked down at his bloodied hands. He shook his head, whipped the reindeer once and shouted, "Yah!" With the ringing of dulled bells and thundering of hooves, they took off again into the pale sky.

He whipped the beasts hard, forcing them to circle round and round Europe. It only took him a few minutes to travel the length of the whole continent. Round and round he went. Germany, Italy, France. But he was only barely clinging to any thread of sanity. They traced the entire Danube in half a minute. He couldn't decide where next to go. Already his blood lust was up again. He felt strong, but perhaps the coat was also intensifying his drives. Shooting across the Prague night sky, his face was fixed into a terrible contortion. A five-year-old Franz Kafka was at his bedroom window, patiently hoping for a glance of St. Nicholas. He gasped as the sleigh flew by and he witnessed that horrifying expression. The image would be repeated to the small boy in many a nightmare. He would never be quite the same again.

Jack had another sudden, lucid thought.

Why limit himself to Europe? He had never been to the *colonies*. What about America? The bright lights. This still relatively *new land*?

It took him less than an hour to cross The Atlantic.

4

It had been freezing, soaring high over the ocean. Actually freezing; as icicles formed underneath the base of the sleigh. But that thick and mottled coat kept him warm. It kept him functioning.

He wasn't even tired. Usually after only a single kill he was simply exhausted. This magical coat was surely an accelerant of extremes. The already kind-hearted Saint Nick had been transformed into a man who was able to actually cross the globe spreading infinite joy and happiness.

But what about himself? He knew he was wicked. What evil could be made with a man already so sinful and so very depraved?

His heart quickened and he let out an excited yelp as he soared over New York's vast harbour. He could barely believe his eyes as he passed close to the colossal Statue of Liberty. Only two years old, he knew all about it, had seen pictures in the broadsheets – but nothing prepared him for the spectacle as he drew up so close.

"My dagger would surely blunt on you," he whispered, before forcing the sleigh down towards the streets.

He found a dark piece of waste ground near to the dry dock and disembarked.

He secured the reins to an oil lamp post and set off in search of his first transatlantic kill. One block away he was thrilled to find three prostitutes. Three bodies soon lay amongst a pile of disregarded rubble. His blood-rusted knife appeared to glisten with darkness in the moonlight. Jack went in search of more victims. Surely the choice of bounty would be plentiful. But the city was too busy, too *alive*. Somewhat dejected, he returned to his seat, whipped the exhausted team once more and tore across the New York sky. On he pressed them, "Somewhere quieter… somewhere barren," he whispered to himself as they ate up hundreds of miles every few seconds. Jack knew there would be many, many opportunities across this great land – he just had to find them. But he must be careful. He was enjoying himself far too much to risk being caught.

While flying over Charlotte, North Carolina, he happened upon a huge field.

A series of large tents were there pitched together, with a menagerie of horses and other animals off to one side. Some kind of circus or travelling roadshow. It appeared as if everyone was asleep, the tents black. Jack landed the sleigh a few metres from the furthest tent.

Before hushing the reindeer, Jack set off quietly on foot towards the first tent. Everywhere was incredibly dark. There was no artificial light emanating from anywhere and the moon was half covered by dark clouds. The fresh country air smelled strange to Jack, something he wasn't used to. He pulled the great coat closer around him. He drew in breath - there was a tantalising aroma of freshly spilled blood. The stench from the animal enclosure was the only other familiar smell to him. He crept up to the tent – about fifteen feet tall, pegged tightly into the ground. As he approached with his knife drawn he read the large red writing up the side: 'Buffalo Bill's Wild West Show.' Clenching the knife between his teeth, he began to unbutton the entrance of the tent. Then he stood there, knife drawn, as his eyes accustomed themselves to the darkness within. There were three Native American women sleeping on camp beds inside. Jack smiled to himself, his eyes sparkling with delight. He plunged his knife into the first woman as she slept. She would never wake again. He sliced through the second's throat before she had a chance to fully wake. Never to know it she was dying in life or in some terrible dream. However, the third woman proved trickier. She began to wake, then shriek as soon as Jack had moved on to the second victim. She scrambled up and bolted towards the exit, screaming at the top of her lungs. Jack lunged after her, sweeping her up off the floor before burying the dagger again and again into her chest. She continued to scream, cut short with terrible wheezing. Then she too was silent.

Jack could hear the commotion beginning in the other tents. He hurried back outside as voices began shouting in the distance and oil lamps were lit.

"Over there!" shouted a voice.

Jack ran frantically towards the sleigh, glancing over his shoulder, a man with a six shooter was in close pursuit. The man stopped to shoot and Jack rolled on his back towards a stack of hay, taking a low wooden fence along with him.

The shot rang out but went wide. Jack scrambled back up, doubled around, screaming in a voice straight from hell, stabbing wildly at the man. The gun was spilled along with the man's blood. Pushing the already dead body to the ground, Jack manically sprinted off towards his team, more footsteps behind him.

"Yah! Yah!" he shouted, as he jumped into the sleigh and grabbed up the reins.

A shot flew past and planted itself in the back of his seat. "Go! Go!"

The spooked reindeer started to run along the grass, away from the tents.

The next to appear on the scene had been Buffalo Bill Cody himself. His six shooter was still smoking. He was a striking image; his hair still brown and hanging long over his wide shoulders. His eyes were piercing; below them a handlebar moustache that connected to a thick goatee beard.

He stopped still and aimed carefully. Jack was already thirty feet in the air. He was turning to look around as Bill's pistol spat out a second bullet. It whistled towards him, glancing off his face. It made a half-inch-deep slice along his right cheek. He screamed in shock, making the reindeer jolt the sleigh upwards. Then a final shot came whizzing towards him. It ripped through the flowing coat, that had formerly belonged to St. Nicholas. It didn't pierce any skin this time, but sent a much more painful shock through him. As he peered gloomily down at the large hole - a burn mark within a green and bloodied coat, his face greyed. It was as if he had been struck and blood was pumping from him. In seconds they were hundreds of miles away.

But his powers were waning. He felt weak.

He knew exactly where his final stop should be.

5

It felt good to be back over London. Scoring the night sky as he approached the Thames, the putrid smell of home below was welcome. Seconds later and he was landing the sleigh on the Upper Ward of the immense gothic structure of Windsor Castle. He staggered along the roof, found a chimney and disappeared down inside it. He landed with a bump and found himself in a small parlour room; gas-lit and expensively decorated. Crucially, it was empty. He scurried along the next corridor. Everywhere was silent.

Not a creature was stirring, not even a mouse.

The Royal Chambers.

He stood outside her room, struggling to keep his balance. He righted himself. He felt wilder than ever before.

He made no noise as he entered the room, closing the door soundlessly behind him.

Inside was pure elegance. There was one small oil lamp on, illuminating the thick red, Chinese wallpaper, the four poster bed, the fine plasterwork and every other chic aspect of the room. As he approached the huge, imposing bed, she did not stir. Queen Victoria of Great Britain and Ireland, Empress of India slept on.

Excitedly, the macabre figure of Jack the Ripper stood over her and leaned down.

"Ho, ho, ho," he whispered.

The monarch's sixty-eight-year-old eyes shot open, instantly awake and alert.

Jack's feral eyes bore into hers.

She stared back, hard.

He withered.

"Eddie," she declared loudly in clipped tones. She sat up on her elbows, "Eddie you look decidedly ghastly. What have you done to yourself this time?"

He took an uncertain step back and Victoria rose up from the mattress, her commanding frame now in a seated position.

"Nothing, Grandmother," he mumbled, fidgeting his hands one over another.

He continued to stumble away from the bed. One hand slipped into his pocket and clutched the blade.

As Victoria's eyes adjusted fully, she took in the full horror of his appearance.

Her eyes narrowed, "Edward, you have been warned before about your… hobbies. This simply will not do."

He looked down at the coat as if it had betrayed him, inching closer to the door.

"Guards!" The Queen hollered.

It made him quiver.

All at once two Royal Guards burst into the room. His knife dropped silently to the floor. It rolled away, hidden on the thick scarlet carpet. They each nodded in turn as they immediately understood the scene.

"You know you have to go back there," Victoria said sternly, swinging her legs off the side of the bed.

"No!" he shrieked.

The guards grabbed him, one by each shoulder.

"They will help you get well again," she said as the guards began leading him out, as he twisted against them.

"No!" he roared even more loudly, being wrenched through the door.

"Merry Christmas for tomorrow, Eddie," she said, as he was dragged away screaming.

Special Dispatch

Angeline Adams & Remco van Straten

The Great War was still a few years away and, while the old way of life was slowly replaced by machines, they were stubborn in the countryside around Belfast. Away from the docks, the rope works and linen mills of the city, the Fair Folk still roamed. At least, that's what Jimmy Corry believed; hadn't his uncle Declan told him so?

Uncle Declan had slept through most of the Christmas morning mass, occasionally prodded by Jimmy when his snoring got too loud, though once outside he was awake as he'd ever been.

"You're disgusting. You've still got the smell of drink on you," Jimmy's ma scolded her younger brother outside the church doors. Jimmy ignored the summons of her stern look to stand defiantly with his uncle.

While his ma and da went home by the church path that led to the farm and surrounding cottages, Uncle Declan liked to take the long way round, through the fields. For him, God didn't live in a building of mortar and stone but in the evening sky, in the rime that lay on a naked field and in the whinny of a horse.

"Did you hear about the warrior under the stone grave there?" Declan pointed at the far end of the field, where a construction of giant stone slabs lay overgrown with gorse.

"One of Cú Chulainn's men. He was buried upright, still sitting on his horse, and around his bony neck he wore a chain with one giant hound's tooth."

Jimmy nodded. His uncle had often told him this, but he didn't mind hearing it again.

Uncle Declan took his big strides through the burnt-off stubble, his gaze down, searching. Jimmy struggled to keep up. He had his eyes down too, though didn't quite know what to look for.

"Here." Uncle Declan suddenly stopped and bent over. "Do you know what this is?"

Jimmy looked at the small object his uncle handed him. "An arrow?"

"Right. But what's so special about it?"

Jimmy let the arrowhead play through his hands. "It's made of stone."

Declan's big calloused fingers closed around the boy's hands.

"Careful, Jimmy boy. Once it's picked up, it must never touch the ground again. Drop it and you'll be dragged away by the Fair Folk."

He laughed his big, rolling laugh. "Right you are, it's made of stone. It's 'cause the Folk can't abide iron and they have to carve everything from stone and wood. Maybe that's why there's not so many of them around anymore. Their stone arrows couldn't compete with our weapons of iron. You won't see as much of the Fair Folk as in the olden days. They tend to keep away from us now and perhaps that's for the best. Nobody's ended up any the better for dealing with them."

Jimmy opened his hand and looked at the small sliver of black flint that lay warm in his palm. His uncle nudged him.

"Stick that in your pocket, Jimmy. To be struck by a fairy dart means death, and a painful one at that. It's good luck to find one, though. I'll bind a bit of string around it so you can wear it for luck. Hide it under your shirt; it's best not to have it out too often, lest the Fair Folk take note of you."

***

Finding the fairy dart had not brought Uncle Declan much good luck in the end, but five years later in that drenched field in France, Jim suspected he himself was only alive because he always wore it. He shouldn't have been there at all at his age and hadn't even given the war much thought until Uncle Declan joined up and told him of the trick.

"So, this young fellow I met, he took a slip of paper and wrote the number eighteen on it. Then he put it in his shoe."

"Why would he do that?"

"Because he asks, the recruiter does, 'Are you over eighteen?' and when you're standing on it, you can swear in truth on it that you *are*." Declan stamped his foot to emphasise his point. "Over eighteen."

The ruse itself seemed silly to Jim, childish even. Yet, it had got him thinking. He was still thinking when word came just a few weeks later that it was time for Uncle Declan to go. And, when he finally decided to join up himself, the recruiting officer took him at his word.

Of course, it broke his ma's heart when he told her at tea that evening. How could it not? She'd wanted to go straight up to the village and tell on him.

"No," his da had said. "The boy's given the King his word, hasn't he? He's going."

"It's Declan who's planted these stupid ideas in his head," said his ma. "Declan the marvelous, Declan the hero. Tell me then, where will Uncle Declan be when my boy gets himself shot in some godforsaken land? Will he be there to give him a Christian burial?"

131

The next morning, Jim's parents were on the platform to see their son off. His da shook his hand and squeezed his shoulder. His ma hugged him and cried and made him promise to be careful.

***

Not even half a year later, of the eleven local lads who'd gone to France, only Jim and Barry, the schoolmaster's son, were left. And Declan, of course. Poor Declan. Jim glanced towards Declan's station as usual whenever he thought of his uncle.

Barry saw him looking and hoisted his mug of muddy tea. "Here's to you, Declan! Merry Christmas!" he called out. There was no answer from where Declan held his lonely vigil, though they knew he'd be grinning.

"Merry Christmas," whispered Jim, glad for once that his voice had been hoarse for days. It hid the catch in his throat and the tears that he could just hold back.

Barry was not the worst when you got to know him better, but he'd always had to look big at Jim's expense, calling him 'our wee Jimmy' and asking him how he'd been doing at school. He knew damn well that Jim had left school the year before to work on the farm and that he didn't write too well. Though the other lads had left school early too, they'd followed suit and 'wee Jimmy' caught on. Never with Uncle Declan though, who'd begun calling him Jim.

"You're a man now, Jim," he'd said. "And men like us, we see a job that needs doing and we do it."

Jim had even swaggered a little, feeling like a man with a future in the army.

All of the others were gone now and though his uncle was still with them, he no longer talked to anyone. Barry, by process of elimination, had become Jim's friend on the Front.

***

132

George was the first of the village boys to go. He'd been too slow and caught lead. One moment they'd heard his wheezing behind them as they ran back to their trench through No Man's Land, then they hadn't.

John Cullen's number came up next. He'd been feverish all week, which in itself was nothing unusual in the trenches, but as he persisted in his duties while growing visibly weaker, the men had begun to look askance at him.

"I think you've proved you're not a shirker, John," Declan said. "You'd better report to the sick bay, for our sakes as well as yours. What if it's contagious?"

"Rot," said Barry. "Trench fever's not contagious." He agreed with Declan, though, and John was whisked away and then he was dead. They buried him in what they called the West Wing, with the other victims of disease. Barry took his boots and his overcoat and shrugged when they told him those were not his to take. John's brother Jacob died just a week later, not of the fever, but of what, nobody could rightly say.

Jacob's death made Jim realise how little changed with the absence of any one man. The weather got colder, the stink of the trench grew pungent and another pair of boots, another overcoat, changed hands. The war churned on, the trench lengthened and even when, in line with Operational Requirements, they had to move and dig a new one, it was still the same trench. Always the same trench.

"This is what Orpheus must've found when he descended into Hades," Barry once complained. "An eternity of freezing water, shit and rats. God, what I would give to have him liven things up a bit here with his harp."

At that, Declan leaped up, grabbed Jim and swung him round. "Come, my darling, let us dance to Orpheus's merry tunes: *Horsie, horsie carry me higher; death's come to fetch me, you'll never get tired.*"

Of course, they themselves had changed. They all wore the military jargon and the rules uneasily at first, like a new Sunday suit that only gets comfortable with repeated use. Underneath their newfound identity as the King's soldiers, they were still fundamentally themselves. Except for Declan. With each explosion, each shower of mud and each bullet that whistled over their heads, Jim saw a bit more of his uncle being torn away. Although Declan still laughed with Barry and the others as before, Jim saw that behind his eyes and smile there was very little left of the man he knew from home.

Nevertheless, Barry was the first to notice that something was seriously amiss with Declan. They hadn't really liked one another at first, until they found that they shared a certain sense of humour. They each hammed their part up and the others took to calling them the Professor and the Fool. Then one day, Declan said something that threw Barry. It was enough to drag Jim out of his own thoughts – and enough for him to realise that, more and more, Declan was talking about 'getting out'.

A 'Blighty wound' was how the English lads put it. Blighty was what they called home and they hoped to get injured badly enough to be sent back there, but not so badly that they couldn't work or father children. Jim and the others joked about it, when a bullet grazed someone's shoulder or whistled past a head.

"Nearly got yourself sent back to the auld sod there," someone would say, and they'd laugh, the near-victim with a tinge of regret or with relief, depending on whether injury or death had been narrowly avoided. Some men took it into their own hands, despite the harsh penalties against self-inflicted wounds. A lad who hadn't been with their section for long, a lanky fellow from Wales who nobody could understand, shot three of his own fingers off. He was "taken away, not sent home," an officer made sure to tell them.

"They must have found powder burns on his other hand," was Barry's guess.

"The big eejit. You've got to be cleverer than that." Jim saw a glint in Declan's eyes that hadn't been there for a long time.

"Oh aye. And you are, I take it?"

"I'd shoot through a sandbag. It'd hide the powder."

Barry scoffed. "Don't be daft. If you've thought of that, so has everyone else. The first thing they'll look for is grains of sand in the wound. They'll take you round the back and shoot you — and not in a way that'll get you sent home! Pull yourself together, man and stop talking like this."

There was a note in Barry's voice that Jim hadn't heard before — as though he knew that nothing he said could have any effect.

Declan just walked away from them with stiff legs and clenched fists. Jim followed and stopped when he saw his uncle's shoulders shake. Declan turned, his eyes wide open, tears trailing through the dirt on his cheeks. He grinned.

"Do you still have the fairy dart, Jim? Just one prick and I'll be ill and none of those butchers will find a mark. They'll not point at me and say, 'Declan Murray, you've harmed yourself.' No, not me. Now, Jimmy lad, give that arrow to me." He reached for it and Jim's hand rose protectively to his chest. Then he stepped back. "No, you keep it. You'll need it more than I do."

Declan's grin had faded. "Tell your ma that I'm sorry for all the hurt I've put her through. Tell your da — well, tell him goodbye from me, will you?"

Before Jim realised what his uncle was doing, Declan was on the fire step, clambering over the top, then running. He heard the rattle of the MG08 and a cry — not a cry really, more a strangled, gurgling exhalation — and he knew Declan wouldn't be back.

***

Declan was still out there now, hanging in the barbed wire, as their constant and slowly deteriorating companion. At times, 'them on the other side' used Declan for target practice. They'd turn their machine gun on him when there was nothing else to shoot at and Declan did his little dance, a parody of life, his stiff limbs jerking against the barbed wire as the bullets tore through him. At first, Barry and Jim had been aghast. Then they got used to it.

"Hear Orpheus playing his harp," Barry said one day when the machine guns started spitting again, cupping his ear.

Jim licked his tobacco paper and finished making his cigarette. "I wish he'd play a different tune, though. Declan just seems to go through the motions."

Barry couldn't believe what was coming out of Jim's mouth. Then a laugh like a cough escaped from him. "He's not much of a dancer, but he'll have to fight the girls off after the war!"

"He's having trouble enough fighting off the rats as it is!"

And that was it, they were off. It was in terrible taste, but sure, wasn't the whole war just that?

Another evening, Barry caught Jim teary-eyed, reading a letter from home.

"Stop crying," he growled. "You don't hear Declan complaining!"

They fell about. It was enough.

***

And that's where they were that Christmas; Barry and Jim in their trench and Declan in his stretch of barbed wire outside. The living had a cup of tea, the corpse had his puddle. A good turf fire, Ma's plum pudding and the Midnight Mass were far away from that field in France. They were stuck in a muddy hole in a muddy field, with mud in their tea and their stew tasting of mud.

They'd already shared most of the edible treats their families had sent between them, before vermin could get to them, and Jim solemnly snapped another biscuit in half while Barry whistled some variation on *God Rest Ye Merry, Gentlemen*. He halted when Jim snorted.

"It's about God putting the Fair Folk to sleep, so Declan told me, just when the nights are longest, like now. When the Folk are at their strongest, you know. 'Let nothing you dismay,' so that they'd not wake baby Jesus." He saw Barry's expression. "I know."

"Your Uncle Declan, Jimmy, is full of shite." Barry rose and cupped his hands around his mouth. "You hear that, Declan? You are full of shite." He sat down again and hoisted his tin mug in front of his face. His voice rose in a fair imitation of Declan's – the Declan from before the war. "But you see, I have to empty this mug – there's an imp at the bottom, so there is, and he's promised me his gold!" He slugged down the last of his tea and laughed.

An answering laughter sounded from the Scottish lads round the curve of the trench – most likely at some joke of their own. Jim's face grew hot, but he said nothing.

Barry too fell silent. He'd caught himself off-guard. Declan was on his mind, the Declan from back home, not the scarecrow that hung there on his silent vigil. "Hey, Jimmy. Tell me about that arrow you're wearing. He gave that to you, didn't he?"

"He did, when I was just a wee boy," Jim grinned, happy to have his mind cast back to those faraway days. He took it from under his shirt and held it so that the light of the lantern could catch it. "It's a fairy dart. It was certain death if they struck you with one, and you mightn't even know it."

"Give us a look, Jimmy. That's not iron, is it?" Barry held out a hand.

"It's stone." Jim lifted the thong over his head and handed it to Barry. "We found it near home. It's good luck to find one. Maybe it was used in the battles between the Folk and men, like when Arthur and Ambrosius came to Ireland to steal the Cauldron of Life."

"Or maybe it's just a flint arrow from prehistoric times, when we were clad in animal skins and hadn't learnt to cast in bronze or iron yet." Barry swatted the thought of fairies away, the arrow still in his hand.

"Careful, now. Once it leaves the soil it mustn't—" Jim's hand shot out, stopping short of grabbing the arrow back. He was, after all, no longer Our Wee Jimmy. Ulster was a long way away, Declan was dead and fairies didn't exist.

"Mustn't what?" Barry said. "More superstition? What did your Uncle Declan tell you would happen? The heavens would rend and the Wild Hunt descend upon us? Or would the ground open under our feet and swallow us? Or ... let's see."

He let go of the stone sliver. It tumbled once, twice. Then, with a small splash, it landed in the wet mud.

Jim stared at it in silence. He'd worn the arrow for half a decade. He'd almost never taken it off, never allowed it to touch the ground. *What am I waiting for? What did I expect?* Barry, too, was silent.

Then the sound came – a high, keening wail.

"You hear that?" Jim said, but Barry was on his feet already, his revolver in his hand. The sound came again, louder now, speaking to Jim in a language that was beyond words, orders, training. All of Declan's stories came back to him at once, especially the sad ones – of the keening woman the really old families used to hear, every time one of them died.

"Jimmy, it's not. I know what you're thinking, but it's not." Barry holstered his revolver and took him by the shoulders. He couldn't have seen Jim mouthing that dreaded name, could he?

"It's that cat, the one those Scots found and kept around for the vermin. Or maybe one of those lads sat on his bagpipes."

Jim nodded, even though he rightly knew that Barry was just talking, saying anything, to prevent that one thought that also tried to crawl into his own head. That one word.

Banshee.

Then it no longer mattered, as a new scream came. They threw themselves down; this was one they were all too familiar with. The mortar flew screeching over their heads and exploded just on the other side of the trench.

"Heavy weather from the east!" Barry yelled. Training and muscle memory took over and they scrambled into position. Jim heard the sound of hooves behind him. He looked round and his hand flew up in reflex against a spray of mud. An elongated mass of blackened bone and matted hair filled the space above him and hooves kicked out so close to Jim's head that they might have dashed his brains out, had Barry not yanked him back. The homely smell of horse washed over Jim.

The horse landed in the trench, churning up the cold mud. It snorted and rolled its eyes and tried to rear, but its rider kept it under control. Then boots splashed in the mud.

The rider patted the animal's flank and whispered in its ear with a raspy voice. The horse was skin stretched over bones, the like of which Jim had only ever seen with sick or mistreated animals. The rider turned and looked down at them. A strangled sound escaped from Jim's throat. It was Declan's face, under the helmet. Declan's face as it had become, with the empty eye sockets, hollow cheeks and the toothy skull-grin. No, this face moved and it spoke.

"'Bout ye, boys! Nice night for it!" The horseman unbuckled his helmet and crouched, the heavy fabric of his overcoat flapping behind him like a pair of wings. The rider's elbows jutted as they came to rest on his knees.

139

Jim had an impression of ribs jutting through pale skin, the abdomen beneath a cavity. He shrugged off the thought. No, of course this wasn't Declan, and what he took for bones were the folds and shadows of fabric.

From closer by, his smile became more human, and Jim could see light in the deep-set eyes. He was gaunt, though. Unnaturally so. The horse moved its head towards its master. Skin and veins stretched over the skull that swung from the thin, sinewy neck. The rider reached behind him to pat the horse's muzzle. His sleeve slid down, revealing the man's knobbly wrist, the twin bones of his lower arm.

"What are you? Cavalry? We thought there were none of you for twenty miles," Barry said, finally. His hand crept to his side arm, and his eyes narrowed. "Are you a messenger? Special Dispatch?"

"Aye. Something like that. Passing through, so I was. I thought: 'There's boys from the Auld Sod. Let's pay them a visit'. Better to be in this hole with you lads, than up there getting a mortar in the bake."

Maybe both he and his horse were very sick, Jim thought. Maybe they were dying of cancer, deemed expendable and sent on dangerous missions. The man produced a stray cigarette and a match.

Barry lunged up and tried to swat the cigarette out of the man's hand. The man effortlessly slid out of Barry's reach, stuck the cigarette in his mouth and struck the match against his boot. In its light, Jim could see just slivers of the man's eyes between his pale lashes. The dark pits of his cheeks expanded as he sucked. He tossed the match away, let a few seconds pass, then smoke steamed from his nose.

"Away with that; we're under attack!" Barry hissed, again making a fruitless feint at the man.

"Are we now? Boyo, listen." The stranger waved his too-thin arm, as if to indicate the entire ravaged landscape of Northern France. "The Germans gave up. Turned themselves in."

He put the palms of his hands together and put his head to rest on them, with his eyes closed. "There's silence now. Like the grave."

It was true, Jim thought. No sounds of men digging themselves out, no coughing, no nothing. *What if everyone else is dead? What if we are dead?* he thought, though he could feel his heart beating in his temples.

The man threw back his head and laughed, a hacking sound churned out by the bobbing Adam's apple in his sunken throat. And with that, Jim again heard the thudding of distant cannons, the rattle of machine guns and the dying of men.

"Just messing with youse. The war's not gone away. Eh, lads, any food? My stomach thinks my throat's been cut!"

Jim shook himself. If he'd died, he could never have invented a fellow like this. All soldiers, the ones who didn't lose their nerve completely, learned to focus on keeping their composure, yet he'd never known anyone to look so relaxed in the wake of such chaos.

"Well? What's that roasting in that pot over there?" The man edged towards the remains of their supper, covered as it was in muck.

Barry planted a foot between him and the food. "There's nothing left."

The man smirked at Barry and shrugged. He turned towards Jim, who recoiled at the stench that came off him. It had to be the cancer that ate him from the inside; the stench of Death lurking around the corner.

"And how about you, soldier? Spare a simple wayfarer a meal?"

"I'll heat up what's left," said Jim. He rose, both because he didn't want to seem inhospitable and because he couldn't bear to be so close to the man. He unearthed the candle that was their only permitted cooking fire, picked up the pot and knocked it against his boot to get the mud off.

The man got up too and brushed off the crates that Barry and Jim had been sitting on earlier. He unbuckled the horse's saddle, hushing the beast as it snorted and tried to step away, and heaved it to the ground to use as a seat for himself.

For a moment he just sat there, in the shelter of the horse's rib cage and hollow belly, facing the two young men. Then he picked something up from the ground and with a wink, handed it to Jim, a wave of his stench moving with him. Jim nodded as he let the stone arrow slide into his pocket. The man rubbed his hands together, retrieved a handkerchief from his coat and lifted the lid of the pot. He leaned over and sniffed loudly.

"Beans. And bacon! What a treat!" He replaced the lid and took the biscuit Jim offered him. Then he sat back and stared at the candle flame as it slowly warmed the sparse meal. "Tell ye what I miss this time of year, lads. It's the Wren Hunt. Christmas always was lean for me, but come St Stephen's Day I'd be at the head of the hunt." He stuck his chin in the air in mock pride, stretching the tendons of his throat. He grinned. "Did youse hunt the Wren?" Saliva had wetted the ruins of his teeth.

"It's not much done in our village anymore," Jim answered. "Once, we stuck some feathers in a potato. People gave us money anyway, so long as they got a feather!"

Jim snorted, half at the memory and half from unease.

"And was there caroling?"

"Aye, and everyone from roundabout would go to the farm, where they'd do their piece. Well, except for my Uncle Declan, who sang like a rooster at dawn. He'd tell a story instead. It was our Barry, here, who put everyone else to shame. Go on, Barry, give us a song." Jim only then realised that Barry hadn't spoken since he'd refused the man his food.

"Yes, Barry, give us a wee song," their guest said, in a tone that Jim didn't like at all. His grin was a leer now. "Or how about a bit of verse. You'll remember this one from school:

'Up the airy mountain, down the rushy glen, we daren't go a-hunting, for fear of little men.'" He clapped the rhythm with his bony hand on his knee.

"Enough of that. Enough of wrens and little men. You're not from Special Dispatch, are you?" Barry rose and raised the revolver that Jim hadn't even seen him draw. He pointed it at the man's head.

"I never said I was." The thin man placed his mug gently on the ground. Ignoring the revolver aimed at his head, he unfolded himself. Jim was struck by how tall he was. In the dark, the horse sniffed and stomped a hoof.

"Who are you?" Barry was shouting now and his revolver trembled.

"Oh Barry, Barry." The man said, with a sigh. "I rode in darkness, when I knew there was folk from home. 'Here,' I thought, 'I could ask for a little food.' But you begrudged me, Barry. If it wasn't for your man Jim here, I'd have starved tonight. Did your ma and da not teach you to treat folk kindly?"

Barry stared at the man in front of him, then started blinking furiously. He steadied the revolver and inhaled deeply.

"No!" Jim lunged at Barry, just as a mortar screamed through the air. His arm hit Barry's and he heard the revolver go off. That was the last thing he knew.

***

The first thing he was aware of was the throat-catching stench of disinfectant, which didn't entirely cover the smell of blood and bowels. He swam back to consciousness in a fever of effort. He wanted to put his arms down by his sides, but found he couldn't. A doctor was with him – not old, but tired-looking.

"They'll mend, Jim," he said, as if they were in the middle of a conversation. He was English. "You've been very, very lucky, Jimmy. Certainly luckier than your friend. I'm afraid he didn't make it. It was a direct hit on your part of the trench, they tell me."

"Special Dispatch," he said, though it wasn't what he wanted to say at all. It took the doctor a while to convince him that there had been only one body with him in the crater that had been their trench. They'd identified Barry, somehow, but of a thin, hungry man and his horse there was not a sign.

"It's all over now, son," said the doctor, with the weary smile of someone who had seen it all before.

"You're going home."

Ellie Bird's Greatest Regret

Stacie Davis

21ˢᵗ December, 1984

Butterflies fluttered in Ellie's stomach as she smoothed down her black rose print tea dress. It was vintage – knee-length and wraparound with three-quarter length sleeves – not at all the style of the Eighties, but she absolutely loved it.

This was her first work Christmas party with AVX and she was a mixture of excitement and fear. Much to her mother's dismay, at twenty-two, Ellie had recently abandoned her sheltered life in the country and moved into her own apartment in Coleraine.

Though right now, she felt very out of her depth as she entered The Queens Arms, a long-standing pub in The Diamond of Coleraine. It was packed with festive party-goers and she was about to lose her nerve and leave when Georgie Morton, AVX's red-haired receptionist, swooped in and rescued her.

The night went by far too quickly. They were joined by a crowd of rowdy construction workers and Ellie ended up sandwiched between Billy and Jonny. Two very witty and charming boys, she had never laughed so much in her life.

Having danced till her feet were sore and sang until she was hoarse, Ellie was ready for home by midnight. She was barely out the door of The Queens Arms when Jonny insisted on walking her home, singing off-key Christmas songs all the way.

When they reached her apartment, Jonny tipped his old-fashioned flat cap and said with a cheeky smile, 'Well, Miss, you are home safe and sound.'

'Yes,' Ellie laughed, fiddling with her keys. 'My very own Christmas saviour.'

'At your service,' Jonny answered with a wink, turning to leave. 'It was very nice to meet you, Ellie Bird.'

'And you, Jonny Simpson.' Ellie tipped her head in a return bow, hoping her disappointment that their brief account was over wasn't written all over her face.

As she put her key in the lock Jonny shuffled about awkwardly, half turning to leave, half staying put. 'Ellie? I just wondered … if …' Jonny stammered nervously, fiddling with the change in his pocket. 'Well … if maybe you would like to go out with me sometime?'

Ellie beamed but quickly reeled herself in before turning round. She was flattered by how anxious he was. 'I would like that. Can we go to see the Christmas lights on Sunday afternoon?'

'OK,' Jonny agreed, a mixture of relief and bemusement. 'Why the Christmas lights?'

'It's something I used to do and haven't done in a while,' she answered thoughtfully, not entirely sure why she had insisted upon it. 'I think it would be a good tradition to start again.'

***

26th December, 1985

Ellie should have been happy; she'd just celebrated her one-year anniversary with Jonny and had a great Christmas, but she was disappointed.

Christmas was her favourite time of year and she had thought, with it being their anniversary as well, Jonny would have proposed. She knew she was being ridiculous; they were happy and they talked about getting married all the time, but she still couldn't help feeling let down.

The more time that passed without a proposal the more disheartened and irritated Ellie became. By Boxing Night in The Railway Arms, Ellie was barely speaking to Jonny, giving him dirty looks across the table and being downright rude.

'Ellie what's going on?' Jonny asked, having coaxed Ellie outside. 'Why are you so angry with me?'

'Why? Really? *Why*?' Ellie hissed, too cross to keep up a pretence. 'Why do you think?'

'I honestly don't know,' Jonny shook his head, utterly baffled. 'It's like you're a completely different person today.'

'Seriously, Jonny, it's not rocket science.' Ellie decided to spell it out for him. Somewhere in the back of her mind she knew she was being unreasonable, but she couldn't stop herself. 'We've been together for over a year, we talk about getting married all the time and I honestly thought you would propose over Christmas but instead my 'big surprise gift' was a bag I really liked from Moores.'

The bag was gorgeous and expensive and Ellie absolutely adored it, but the most important thing in the world to her was spending her life with Jonny and she couldn't help resenting the gift as some sort of consolation prize.

'But … you loved that bag. You pointed it out every time we walked by …' Jonny stuttered, feeling wrong-footed and confused. He loved Ellie. She was the only one for him and he did plan to propose to her at some point, he just hadn't planned to do it right now. Nor had he realised he had been *meant* to do it right now. 'Ellie, I love you and we *will* get married, but I really don't see what the rush is?'

'No, I guess there isn't a rush,' Ellie replied sharply, in a tone which could cut like a knife. 'Why on earth would you be in a rush to spend the rest of your life with the person you love?'

Ellie was so furious she didn't give Jonny time to respond. Turning on her heel, she stormed off, straight across the road, without looking.

The last thing she saw were the headlights coming towards her.

***

21st December, 1989

It had been a few years, but not much had changed. Ellie wandered the streets of Coleraine, lost in happy memories while trying to ignore the ever-present sense of regret. Admiring the Christmas decorations in the store windows and attempting to get carried away in the Christmas spirit, she felt lost and a long way from home.

She missed home.

Standing outside Dixons department store admiring a beautiful but very impractical pair of shoes that she could never afford, she heard a familiar laugh. It had been a while, but she would know his laugh anywhere. And sure enough, as she turned, there he was, *her Jonny*.

Her Jonny, in his faded, dirt-covered jeans, old-fashioned flat cap and worn jacket. Hands in his pockets, head cocked to one side with an *'up to no good'* smirk playing on his lips as he walked down the street next to Billy. Good old funny Billy Reed, stocky and sweet, he could keep a nation going.

Ellie felt the warmth of familiarity clash with the sense of loss and longing.

'Come on Jonny,' Billy pleaded as they drew closer. 'We have to go to The Ploughman later, it's the girls from Dixons Christmas party.'

'There's no way I'm going there to be stuck in the middle of a group of giggling girls,' Jonny replied, shaking his head. 'Not a chance, mate. You're on your own.'

'But Marie said she'd be there,' Billy pleaded, stopping Jonny in the middle of the street to make his point. They were only a few feet from where Ellie stood frozen to the spot. 'And you know Marie and I have had a flirty thing going on.'

Jonny eyed Billy sceptically. He may have had a flirty thing going on with Marie, but Jonny wasn't so sure Marie felt the same way.

'Besides,' Billy continued, seeing his opening when Jonny didn't immediately protest. 'She might have a few fit mates and you know you could …'

Jonny's playful look turned to thunder in an instant. 'I could what?' He asked in a steely tone.

'Nothing, mate,' Billy said quickly, sighing in defeat. 'It just, it's been a few years. I thought you might want to get back out there. But never mind.'

Four years, it has been almost four years, Jonny thought angrily, his gaze briefly flitting upwards to behind Billy's head. *Since Ellie …*

Ellie saw Jonny's gaze shift and she panicked, quickly moving into the open doorway before it could land on her.

Jonny was about to look back to Billy when something caught his eye just in front of Dixon's window. He could have sworn he saw … *Was it Ellie? It couldn't have been, could it?* He stared in disbelief at the empty space. *Perhaps Billy was right. Perhaps he did need to move on.*

***

16ᵗʰ December, 1992

Ellie stared in horror at the derelict street. She couldn't believe the Troubles had resulted in this. So many of the shops she had visited regularly were just – gone. Burnt out and destroyed. Who knew a car bomb could cause this much damage?

She was so fixated on the demolished town centre that it was several minutes before she noticed the construction worker removing debris into a large skip. He was a little older, with a few laughter lines starting to show, but it was still him. *Her Jonny.*

She watched him work rhythmically, his strong frame making light work of the rubble. She considered calling out to him but before she could, she heard someone else call his name.

'Jonny? Jonny?' A tall thin-faced girl with long dark hair hanging down below a knitted hat called insistently from Ellie's right. The girl looked familiar, but Ellie couldn't quite place her.

Jonny looked up and smiled but it didn't reach his eyes. 'Hi Marie,' he said politely as he walked towards her. 'How are you?'

'I'm great,' Marie answered brightly, moving in to give Jonny a hug, which he awkwardly returned. 'I was just getting a few bits for Ma, so I brought you a flask of tea and some chocolate digestives to warm you up.'

'That was kind of you Marie,' Jonny replied, taking the plastic bag. To make conversation, he added, 'It's sad to see the town in this state, isn't it?'

Marie? Marie? Ellie thought, regret and jealousy swirling round her stomach as Marie and Jonny chatted. *How did she know Marie?*

Then it dawned on her. This was the same Marie who worked in Dixons. The same Marie that Billy had been so desperate to go out that night and bump into. Ellie didn't really know her but had met her in passing a few times. She had seemed nice.

Now, though, Ellie wasn't sure she liked Marie at all, especially she was bringing *her Jonny* tea and biscuits. What had happened that night? Marie obviously couldn't be seeing Billy if she was visiting Jonny like this.

Ellie restrained herself from casually walking over and ruining their cosy little get-together. It may have been a number of years since he had officially been *her Jonny,* but she had never forgotten him. *She* hadn't moved on and found somebody else.

But perhaps he had … The unwanted thought filled Ellie's head, rooting sadness deep into her soul. She turned away from Jonny and Marie, staring back at the demolished building, feeling more broken than it could ever be.

***

13th December, 1997

Cosied up enjoying the warmth, Ellie sat tucked away in the back corner of her favourite Coleraine Café, Heralds at 22. The café had received a shiny new makeover since the bombing in 1992 and was a welcome escape from the bitter cold rainy weather outside.

The back corner was the perfect place to people watch and relax without being disturbed. Ellie eavesdropped as a mother and daughter chatted and laughed while they sorted through Christmas presents at a nearby table.

Further down the shop, opposite the counter, an elderly gentleman nursed a cup of coffee and a pastry. Taking a small square box from a plastic bag, he set it lovingly in the centre of table. The wrapping was exquisite, luxury paper covered in small delicate Christmas trees, finished off with a thick red ribbon. Ellie guessed it had been professionally wrapped in the shop where he'd bought it.

Not long after, an older lady appeared, wearing a long coat and a thick cosy-looking scarf. The elderly gentleman nodded to the waitress behind the counter, who brought down a pot of tea and another pastry as the older lady took the seat opposite him.

Ellie was so consumed with watching the love between the older couple, and the joy on the women's face when she opened the present and found a delicate gold brooch, that she didn't notice the man and young girl who had taken the table nearby.

The man had his back to her and the little girl, Ellie presumed she was about three, was laughing as they played with her toy ponies. Ellie couldn't help but smile at the child's infectious joy. The little girl looked up and smiled back at her. Noticing the gesture, the man with her turned, bemused, to see who she was smiling at.

Ellie recognised him immediately – *her Jonny*. He looked more distinguished now and was greying slightly around the temples, his frame a little fuller, but he was still as handsome as ever. Ellie shrunk quickly back into the shadows, out of sight.

The warmth and love she had been feeling turned to ice as she contemplated the possibility that Jonny and Marie had married and this was their child.

***

31ˢᵗ December, 1999

It was the night the whole world had been waiting for, with equal amounts of excitement and fear. The Millennium was here, well almost, and Ellie was going to bring it in in style. She hadn't celebrated a New Year in a long time, but this was going to be the start of a whole new century and there was no way she was missing out on that.

In The Railway Arms, Ellie flitted round the room all night, dancing, laughing, singing and partaking in all of the craic. Just before midnight, the whole bar counted down and the roar of 'Happy New Year' as the clock struck twelve was deafening.

She had the best night ever and when Ellie spilled out on to the street with the other patrons, she was floating on air. A little way further down, on the opposite side of the road, she spotted two men sitting on a bench. *Her Jonny* and Billy were in deep conversation.

Crossing the street, Ellie casually leaned against a lamp post and pretended to look in her handbag.

'It's a whole new year and a new century, mate,' Billy said joyously. They had clearly had a few drinks. 'Time for a change, well, two big changes.'

'Exciting times,' Jonny replied with a huge smile. 'Though you're completely outnumbered now.'

'Aw man, I don't care,' Billy replied, hand on heart. 'Claire and I waited so long for this and now both our girls are here safe and sound, our little Millennium miracles.'

'I know, I really am pleased for you both,' said Jonny, clapping Billy on the back, although there was a sadness in his eyes. 'If not a little envious.'

'Ach, there's still time for you,' Billy told him with gusto. 'You only need to get out there. The right girl is just around the corner.'

'I don't know, Billy,' Jonny answered sadly. 'The years are ticking on. I can't imagine there being anyone else who'll be the right fit for me.'

'I know, mate,' said Billy, knowing exactly who Jonny was thinking about. 'But …'

Ellie turned on her heel and fled. She couldn't listen to any more. The pain was just too much. Her joyous high sunk like a lead balloon.

***

9th December, 2008

153

The Causeway Hospital was a different place at the dead of night. Still and eerily quiet. Ellie never had much cause to visit it, but the grounds were beautiful for walking through, especially in the moonlight and tonight, Ellie needed to walk.

Today had felt restless. It had been cloudy and wet, typical December weather, but also unsettled in a way that Ellie couldn't quite put her finger on, as if something awful was about to happen.

Apart from some low-level lighting inside and a few floodlights outside, the hospital was pretty much in darkness, though a large Christmas tree with twinkling lights was visible in the lobby. Rounding the corner towards the Accident and Emergency entrance, Ellie stopped in her tracks as she noticed a woman fleeing through the doors, followed closely by a man.

'Margaret, wait,' Jonny pleaded, catching up with her at the pay station. 'I know this is hard but please don't leave.'

'I'm sorry, Jonny,' said Margaret, clearly distressed. 'I know she's our mother and she's dying, but I can't sit there pretending to be a doting daughter when really, she stopped being my mother a long time ago.'

Jonny tried to speak but Margaret cut him off, holding up her hands. 'And don't even get me started on saint Sarah's attitude and her little digs.'

'I know she hasn't been easy to live with and you know I don't agree with how she treated you when you found out you were pregnant,' Jonny reasoned, taking hold of Margaret's shoulders. 'And Sarah has always been a spoiled brat but,' Jonny's voice went quiet. 'She *is* our mother and these are her last moments. You should be here for that; for yourself – for closure.'

Margaret crumpled into Jonny. Despite her strong exterior she was actually rather soft-hearted on the inside. Ellie's heart broke a little as she watched them go back into the hospital.

It was never easy to lose somebody. She wished she could be there for *her Jonny* in the days and weeks to come.

With a heavy heart, Ellie walked away.

***

14th December, 2012

The festive spirit was in full force throughout the Diamond Shopping Centre, with beautiful decorations, Christmas trees and dressed-up store windows. Ellie watched the kids excitedly lining up for Santa's grotto, before going downstairs to skate on the indoor ice-rink.

The shopping centre had been intended to 'put Coleraine on the map' and compete with the likes of Fairhill in Ballymena and Foyleside in Londonderry, but it had never really taken off. It had several good shops but still, many units lay empty.

A lot of shops in Coleraine seem to have disappeared, Ellie thought, taking the escalator up to the food court. *Coleraine just isn't the town it used to be. Maybe it's time to move on to somewhere new,* she wondered sadly, as she found a seat near the large corner windows overlooking the old bridge and the new Dunnes Stores.

A few tables over, Ellie recognised Jonny's sister, Margaret, setting down a tray full of food. She was followed by a slightly younger girl who looked remarkably like her, presumably, her daughter. The girl was wearing a huge 18th birthday badge which, to Ellie's surprise, she seemed to be in good humour about.

'Thanks for this fantastic badge, Uncle Jonny,' the girl laughed, pressing it so it flashed and played music.

Of course, Ellie thought with a knowing smile. *That was typical Jonny humour.*

'It'll be great for getting free birthday drinks in Kelly's later!' She smiled cheekily.

'You're very welcome, Lily.' Jonny smiled, tipping his old-fashioned flat cap in an all too familiar move. 'Now, put on your princess tiara while I pretend that you're not actually old enough to go to places like Kelly's.'

Lily obediently pulled the plastic silver tiara, complete with pink fur and large fake gems, out of a shopping bag. She planted it firmly on her head, giving a huge thumbs-up to her uncle.

'You really do look quite the picture, Lily.' Margaret laughed, shaking her head. 'You're far more like your uncle than you'll ever be like me. That's just the kind of eejit activities that he'd be up to.'

Ellie felt a lump rise in her throat as she remembered all of Jonny's fun-loving antics, especially the Halloween pumpkin hat he'd fashioned out of some tinfoil and orange emulsion. Ellie still had no idea where he'd found orange emulsion.

'Well, Margaret, Lily and I just like to bring laughter and sunshine into the lives of those around us,' Jonny answered seriously. He indicated the standoffish woman at the other end of the table who was staring uninterestedly at her phone, adding, 'Though clearly we need to work a bit harder on Sarah.'

Ellie had never had very much interaction with Sarah. She was spoiled and not in a good way. Sarah had been about Lily's age when Ellie had been dating Jonny. It would appear she hadn't lost her attitude over the years.

Lily and Jonny exchanged a look of mischief before breaking into a very loud chorus of *'Happy Birthday'* as Lily placed the tiara on Sarah's head.

'You two are ridiculous!' Sarah said sharply, slamming the tiara on the table and storming off.

'Auntie Sarah really takes things way too seriously.' Lily chuckled as she and Jonny dissolved into giggles.

Margaret tried to give them a telling-off but she was struggling to hide her own smile.

***

1st December, 2019

As dusk started to fall in Coleraine town centre the lights twinkled brightly, all white and blue sparkle. The Caring Caretaker, dressed up like Santa and collecting for charity as he always did in the run-up to Christmas Eve, was tucked up in his hut as people milled about.

Ellie sat on one of the decorative benches near the Town Hall. The town centre was vastly different now, compared to when she had been young. There were more coffee shops than clothes shops, more people busy rushing about, and some sort of virus was on the loose that had people starting to worry.

Even the basic benches had been replaced by these modern stone and metal ornamental ones. Which looked great, but they were cold and hard, not at all comfortable for sitting on for longer than a few minutes.

This was the first Sunday after the big Christmas lights switch-on ceremony. It was Ellie's favourite time to come and see the Christmas décor, away from the crowds, giving her peace to just soak it all in.

She watched as an older man sat down stiffly on the bench opposite her, an empty flowerbed between them. He seemed frail and was assisted by a woman in her twenties, who Ellie assumed was probably his daughter.

'Are you sure you're OK, Uncle Jonny?' Ellie heard the girl fuss as she perched on the seat next to him.

Spinning round to take a closer look at the man, Ellie couldn't believe it. It was him, *her Jonny*, but he was a shadow of his former self, breathless, with greying skin and sunken eyes. He looked exhausted.

'Yes, Lily, I'm OK,' Jonny answered softly, with a kind smile. 'Thank you for bringing me to see the lights.'

'It's no problem, Uncle Jonny,' said Lily, smiling warmly as she squeezed his hand. 'I know you like to come every year and soak up the Christmas spirit.'

'Unfortunately, I fear this might be my last year,' Jonny replied quietly, looking into the distance. 'But I still remember the first Sunday I sat here. It was my first date with Ellie …'

Lily squeezed his hand a little tighter as a tear rolled down her cheek. Ellie froze, instantly transported back to that time as Jonny reminisced.

'She was the most beautiful girl I'd ever seen. I couldn't believe my luck when she agreed to go out with me, but she was insistent that we come into the town centre and see the Christmas lights,' Jonny explained, lost in a memory. 'She always went to see the lights and store window decorations with her grandmother.'

'You were the first person I invited along with me after my gran was gone,' Ellie whispered, as Jonny smiled knowingly and nodded.

'We had the best time sitting on a bench, people watching, making up stories for the lives of strangers and laughing.' Jonny closed his eyes and sighed deeply. 'We were always laughing. That's what I miss the most.'

'Me too,' Ellie breathed, as a tear escaped from Jonny's eye.

'You really loved her,' Lily said in awe, tears flowing freely. 'There was never anyone else for you, was there Uncle Jonny?'

'No,' Jonny told her firmly, as Lily dried her eyes. 'She is my one and only.'

'And you are mine.' Ellie whispered regrettably, drying her own eyes.

'I hope I find a love like that,' said Lily, clearing her throat as she stood up. 'I'll go get us a coffee.'

Jonny nodded as Lily walked away. Then he looked over to where Ellie sat, on the opposite side of the flower bed, and whispered. 'I'll see you soon, my love.'

***

24th December, 2019

Ellie waited impatiently. She had been waiting for a while, on the same bench where she last saw him and he'd seen her. It was almost midnight on Christmas Eve. The town centre was deserted and there was a mizzle of rain.

They didn't have plans to meet but she had a feeling he would be here tonight, that this would be the night the stars would align and they would finally be together. She really wished he'd hurry up.

Eventually, a figure appeared, walking casually towards her. He was younger, exactly how she remembered him. The frail old man had been replaced by the handsome young man in his faded jeans and old-fashioned flat cap.

'I thought I'd find you here.' Jonny smiled. He looked like a naughty schoolboy, hands in his pockets, with an 'up to no good' look about him, just as he always had. The loveable rogue.

'Oh, really?' said Ellie, trying to sound as cross as possible. 'Why is that? Do you think I have nothing else to do but wait for you?'

'I hope not,' Jonny answered, taking a seat beside her. 'I've been waiting for you for an extremely long time.'

'Really?' Ellie gave him a disbelieving look, though she knew in her heart it was true. 'So, what took you so long?'

'Life … Love … Death …' He replied with a resigned shrug. 'I guess mine was just a slower path.'

'You always did like taking the long way home.' Ellie gave a sad half-smile, staring straight ahead as she recalled the memories of their time together so many years ago.

'Yes,' Jonny agreed, following her gaze into the distance. 'But I liked it a lot better with you.'

'I waited for you,' Ellie whispered, a tear slipping down her cheek. 'I always waited.'

Jonny took her hand, turning Ellie around to face him. Her heart melted as she looked into his chocolate-brown eyes and he whispered, 'I'm really glad you did.'

As they kissed, the years of waiting, sadness and regret fell away like a flutter of snowflakes, their souls reunited at last as a blinding light spirited them away.

Secret Santa

Morna Sullivan

Henry loved everything about Christmas. He made the season stretch all year. In January he hunted for Christmas wrapping paper and crackers reduced in the sales. He bought Christmas presents throughout the year. He made his Christmas cards in the summer and began organising the office Christmas dinner in August. He put up his tree on 1st November and started writing his Christmas cards later that month. He organised the office Secret Santa in December and planned and hosted the family dinner and get together on the day itself.

He had never lost his childlike innocence and excitement of the festival and his work colleagues in the Anderson and Murdoch sales office were secretly relieved that they weren't asked to organise the office Christmas party each year.

It was a thankless task and yet Henry embraced it with vigour, joy and enthusiasm, as he did with most jobs, announcing, before Prue had bought her children's new school uniforms that it was time to think of this year's party.

Jolene was thankful they had Henry. Every office needed someone just like him to think of where they might go for dinner, design the seating plan and deal with complaints on the day. She admired how Henry coped with all these issues gracefully, never complaining, always smiling and agreeing to take on board suggestions for next year, to make it even better. Managing this team certainly brought her daily challenges. If only everyone could be a bit more like Henry, especially Kathy. She seemed to find fault with everything, including Henry's chirpy emails that announced Christmas was approaching.

14th August

Colleagues

We've reached that wonderful time of the year again, when it's time to think of the Christmas party! Are you excited yet? Only 130 days to go ☺

The time: Friday 22nd December

The place: YOU decide

I don't want to step on anyone's toes, so if anyone else would like to organise the party this year, let me know – happy to step aside – or to step up and do it once more. As always I'm happy to consider suggestions for this year's venue, but to kick the discussion off I'm suggesting O'Malley's (just for a change!), the new Italian in The Bridges centre, Veni, Vidi, Vici (there's been great reports in the paper) and the Victoria Hotel (if we're feeling flush!) Their entertainment looks good. Anyway, please vote using the buttons at the top of the email by this Friday to let me know your preference or suggest other choices. Menus are attached for all three venues.

Ciao for now

Henry

PS (I've let slip my preference, haven't I??)

Later that day, round the tea point everyone had an opinion about where might be a better Christmas dinner venue, but no one wanted to take the task off Henry's hands.

"Thanks for the reminder I need to buy the school shoes Henry. Have you thought of The Old Keys Inn? Martin's works do was there last year. He loved it, might be worth a try … but all your ideas sound fine to me," said Prue.

"It's good. And so's The Park, but all those you've suggested have good bars and good food – what more do we need?" asked Sean.

"I like something less traditional. You get fed up with turkey, don't you? A Chinese banquet might be good for a change – but I like the sound of Veni, Vidi, Vici." Jolene smiled at Henry.

"Well, it's up to all of you. You know I'm happy to go anywhere – and happy to organise it unless someone else wants to," he replied.

"What about the buffet at the Riverside Hotel? It's great value." Kathy pushed her way past him to grab milk out of the fridge. "The Victoria Hotel seems a bit pricey for what you get – well they all are – but they all stick on an extra tenner for the privilege of being squashed round a table at Christmas. And I wouldn't go back to O'Malley's. My main course was awful last year and the portions were small. It's really not worth the money."

"It wasn't that bad, Kathy – you maybe made the wrong choice. My salmon was good. See if they'll throw in cocktails and get a good deal for us," said Prue.

"I'll see what I can do. I want it to be even better than last year's. Don't forget to vote!"

Henry counted down the days to Christmas on a spreadsheet every year which included the strict timetable he adhered to in planning his Christmas traditions – the countdown to when his Christmas tree went up, when he wrote and posted his Christmas cards. When he baked his Christmas cake, when he wrapped his Christmas presents, when he started watching Christmas films, when it was acceptable to begin listening to Christmas music, when he organised the Christmas jumper charity day in work, and his favourite event of all, when he organised the office Secret Santa.

21st August
Colleagues
The results are in! Thanks for the responses.
I'm happy to organise the event again this year and can reveal that we will be going to Veni, Vidi, Vici on 22nd December!!
I'll be round to collect your £10 deposits this week.
(And of course we'll be having the Secret Santa before we go for dinner that day!)
Grazie
Henry

Jolene watched as Henry updated his spreadsheet first with the deposits paid, then in November with the menu choices selected. His part in the operation always ran like clockwork. The others might whinge about the venue, but she knew once they were there and had consumed a few drinks it would all be fine.

Henry would print off their menu choices like he always did as Kathy would no doubt argue about what she had ordered. For many years Henry seemed to end up eating something different to what he had selected. Rather than make a fuss, he ate the unwanted meal that no one could remember ordering, despite everyone knowing he had printed off their choices. He enjoyed it, smiling and saying it was really the best choice on the menu. He was determined nothing would spoil the Christmas cheer for anyone.

Friday 1st December (as well as being the day Henry opened his chocolate advent calendars at home and in the office) was traditionally the day Henry began to organise the Secret Santa. As the Christmas month commenced, he embraced the festive spirit fully, each day wearing a different Christmas tie to work. As Christmas Day drew closer his ties became more flamboyant. Friday's tie was a small repeating pattern of understated robins on a spruce green background.

He was the first person to arrive in the office that morning. By the time everyone else had appeared he had already assembled the office Christmas tree, (another task no one ever wanted to do) decorated everyone's desk with tinsel and deposited a handmade Christmas card on their desk.

By the time they had all sat down at their desks, admired or complained about the shade of tinsel and opened their first Christmas card, Henry was already sipping his second cup of tea of the morning from his red reindeer mug. And by the time they'd switched on their computers his email about Secret Santa was already waiting for them in their in-boxes:

1st December

Colleagues

Are you as excited as I am?? Today I'm delighted to kick off proceedings for this year's Secret Santa! You know the rules. £15 max spend, something fun and festive (it is Christmas!) and something practical. All presents to be wrapped, labelled and delivered to the box under the Christmas tree in the office before our dinner on 22nd December (three weeks today!!)

Let me know if you're taking part by lunchtime today so you can pick the name of your Secret Santa recipient and start thinking of what you're going to get them.

The more the merrier (Christmas).

This will be the sign the party has well and truly started!

Henry

Kathy sighed and slammed her mug on her desk so firmly she spilled tea on the files she was working on and the newly attached tinsel fell off her monitor.

"What a waste of money! It would be better giving it all to charity."

"Well why don't you do that?" Sean asked.

"I might. It would make more sense. When I think of some of the things I've got in Secret Santas over the years. They usually end up in charity shops and sometimes I think that's where they've originated too," said Kathy.

"What's wrong with that? I'm all for recycling!" said Sean.

"No pressure for anyone to take part." Henry wheeled round in his chair. "We could go back to £10 limit like last year. If it helps?"

Kathy sniffed.

"Sure it's just a bit of a laugh," said Prue. "Do you remember those Christmas washing up gloves I got last year? I never used them, but you should have seen Martin and the kids wearing them on Christmas Day."

"Glad you liked them," said Henry. "A bit of frivolity and something useful – you know the rules!"

"So it was you! The prosecco truffles were delicious," Prue smiled.

"My lips are sealed!" said Henry.

"I still love those elf slippers I got a couple of years ago," said Jolene.

"I got rose scented coat hangers last year," said Henry. "Not sure everyone understood the rules! But I recycled them and my gran liked them so all was not lost!"

"I don't know who thought last year I'd ever wear a plum pudding bobble hat," said Kathy.

"You know the rules, Kathy, we couldn't possibly say!" smirked Sean. "You'll maybe get a matching scarf this year!"

"That would be a complete waste of money," she replied.

"It'll be good fun. Just a bit of Christmas cheer. It wouldn't be the same without you, Kathy," said Jolene. "A tenner should be plenty."

"Let me know what you decide by lunchtime and we can pick the names out of the hat later!" Henry said.

At lunchtime Henry scrunched up small pieces of paper with everyone's name written on them and summoned them to pick their Secret Santa recipient from his reindeer mug.

"You know the rules. If you get your own name, put it back and choose again."

Kathy selected her piece of paper. "Oh it's mine!" she screwed the paper up and put it back into the reindeer mug.

"Better luck next time!" said Henry swishing them round.

Kathy dipped her hand in a second time and took out a piece of paper, unrolled it. "That should be easy!" She folded it up again and held it tight in her clenched fist.

Sean rubbed his bald head when he opened his. "I may need to do some research here."

As usual Jolene gave little away when she opened hers. "I'll eat this later," she smiled and slid the crumpled paper into her skirt pocket.

When he came to Prue, she selected hers, opened and laughed, "Fantastic! I'll have fun with this one!"

"And the last one is mine!" Henry unrolled the paper and smiled. "Great! That's us all sorted. Let's hope you all get something good. Remember it's a bit of fun. I can't wait until the 22nd to see what everyone gets. I know what I'm getting mine already – and they'll love it. I've seen it online. I'll remind you closer to the time to bring them in and don't forget to label them. Happy shopping!" Henry returned to his turkey and stuffing sandwich and started trawling the internet to make his purchase.

As promised, he sent out regular emails reminding everyone about their Secret Santa purchases as well as Christmas jumper day and the Christmas dinner. Most lunchtimes after browsing the local shops for new decorations and spotting bargains for his colleagues, he picked up his daily Christmas sandwich and spiced apple drink from the deli next door (obligatory in December) and returned to the office to share his new knowledge.

On Monday, sporting a blue tie with a skiing snowman, he told Sean, "There's 20% off all perfume in McDougall's chemist today and tomorrow if you need anything for Margaret. I got aftershave for Joe there today. And there's three for two on all toys in M and J Black's all week," he told Jolene.

"Thanks Henry!" said Jolene.

"There's 20% off partywear in Nouveau if you haven't got your new outfit for the dinner yet," he told Prue.

"Oh I must take a look. I've nothing to wear," giggled Prue.

"Any bargains in bookstores?" Kathy asked.

"Haven't seen any yet – but I'll keep looking and let you know."

Kathy cleared her throat. "I'd love that new cookbook by Barry McKnight. You know the one that goes with his new TV programme?"

"Maybe Secret Santa will get it for you," said Sean.

"You'll be wishing you'd kept the £15 limit. It's on offer in SuperFoods at £14.99 – you'll not get it for a tenner," said Jolene.

"It'll be cheaper online," said Kathy.

"Let me know if it is. I might get it for my sister. She loves him," said Prue.

"Don't see any offers yet. Too popular I'd say," said Henry munching his Wensleydale and cranberry sandwich as he trawled the internet at his desk. "But I'll keep an eye out for you."

Each day Henry monitored the arrival of any presents in the large cardboard box he'd decorated in silver snowman patterned wrapping paper and left under the Christmas tree. Each week he sent out jolly reminders.

Then on the Thursday afternoon, wearing his red tie with the Christmas tree that lit up, he sent a final reminder.

Colleagues
Last call for Secret Santa gifts. You need to deposit them under the tree by 10.00am tomorrow. I don't know about you, but I can't wait to see what we all get ☺. And I can't wait to go to Veni, Vidi, Vici. See you tomorrow in your glad rags!
Ciao
Henry

That evening, as Jolene was clearing away the dishes from the dinner table her mobile phone rang.

"Hi Jolene, I'm in hospital. In A & E. I'm ok."

"What's happened?"

"I got knocked off my bike on the way home. I've a fractured ankle. I'm a bit woozy, but otherwise I'm fine. I'll not be in tomorrow, or probably this side of Christmas."

"Ach Henry! You'll miss everything!"

"I know, I know…" his voice wavered.

"It couldn't be a worse time for you. Did you get the details of who knocked you off the bike?"

"No. It all happened so fast. All I remember is a loud bang and when I woke up, I was in hospital. It's a hit and run."

"Any witnesses?"

"Yes – the police said a couple of people have said it was someone in a silver car apparently. They sped off after hitting me."

"How could anyone do that?"

"I guess they panicked. They'd have known they hit me."

"That's awful. Is it sore?"

170

"Not at the moment, but I'm drugged to the eyeballs with pain relief. It'll be sore when that wears off and I try to walk on it."

"It won't be the same without you tomorrow and on the run up to Christmas… it's not Christmas without you… But as long as you're ok, that's all that matters. We can celebrate again when you're better. Is Joe with you?"

"Yea. He's been great. I'm in good hands. I'm going to have to supervise him in the kitchen, giving him orders for things I can't do. We'll still manage to host Christmas Day – I'd hate to disappoint them – my gran and mum and Bill and Joe's mum and dad have been looking forward to it since last year!"

"Well take it easy."

"The timing just sucks. I was so looking forward to the dinner tomorrow and of course Secret Santa. I was going to wear my new tie Joe bought me. It plays 'Rudolph the Red Nosed Reindeer' when you press his red nose and it lights up. It's the best one yet!"

"Ach Henry. I know, but it sounds like you've been lucky, it could've been so much worse. You could've been killed! I hope they get who hit you. They deserve to be locked up. It's despicable. Cowardly. But you'll not be doing much dancing this Christmas."

"I know – I'll miss the dancing tomorrow night. I've printed off the menus and everything for tomorrow – they're in my drawer."

"You're so organised! No one could do that job as well as you. We'll miss you tomorrow so much!"

"I'll miss you all… too…" Henry's voice faltered again.

"Take it easy and stay off that leg until it heals properly. Remember – no dancing! Take care, Henry. Speak soon. Bye."

The next morning Henry's colleagues were surprised that he wasn't the first one to arrive in the office.

"It's not like him to be in late," said Sean.

"He's probably getting some last-minute Christmas surprise for us," said Prue.

"He's probably still deciding which one of those hideous ties to wear," said Kathy.

"Leave him alone will you? Sure it's just a bit of fun – he's not doing anyone any harm," said Sean.

Kathy reddened.

Jolene called them together.

"That's awful! Who would drive off after hitting someone?" asked Sean when Jolene told them all about Henry's accident.

"I'm sure he's devastated at missing everything today. He lives for this day all year. And he's put so much work into it as usual," said Prue.

"He is gutted but he said he wanted us to go ahead with everything," said Jolene.

"Let's hope he's got everything organised properly for us," said Kathy.

Everyone glared at her.

"Of course he has Kathy! I've got the paperwork for the Christmas dinner booking so we'll be ok. He always thinks of everything and everyone – if only everyone else would! We'll just have to go out again after Christmas when he's back to work," said Jolene.

"Better get started on this Secret Santa now. Henry will be desperate to know what everyone gets." Prue gathered everyone round the Christmas tree to commence the giving of gifts. She lifted the first present out, read the label, called out Sean's name and handed the red and silver striped wrapped package to him. He tore open the paper to uncover a pair of black socks with robins on them. At the ankle joint on one sock was a concealed button, which, when pressed played Jingle Bells.

"Fantastic! Just what I need!" he laughed, "and this is even better." He shook a box of whiskey fudge. "Thanks Santa!"

"Mine's next!" Prue held the gift tag on a pink and gold sparkly gift bag and lifted out a pink tissue-wrapped package. She unfolded the paper gently to reveal a small black box and a bag of scented bath bombs. She opened the box to find a pair of white and silver snowflake earrings with diamantés in the middle. "Oh! These are perfect – they'll be great with this dress! Thanks Santa!"

"You're next, Jolene!" Prue handed her a parcel wrapped in green paper covered in silver Christmas trees topped off with a large silver bow. Jolene tore off the paper to discover a gold box. She opened it to find a Christmas tree brooch decorated with red and blue baubles and a sparkly gold star. When she flicked the switch at the back of the brooch tiny lights flashed.

"I love it!" she cried. She delved into the parcel wrapping to find a poinsettia patterned mug cradling a bag of mini marshmallows and a sachet of drinking chocolate. "Someone knows me very well! Thanks Santa!" said Jolene.

Kathy rolled her eyes.

173

"Just two parcels left!" said Prue. "This one's for Henry." She lifted out a parcel wrapped in brussels sprout patterned paper." We'll keep it here until he returns. He would have loved all the gifts and he'd be proud of us all for sticking to his rules. We'll have to get pics of them and send them to him. It'll cheer him up. He always loves trying to guess who bought what. So, last but not least, here's yours, Kathy."

Kathy reddened as she took the oblong shaped parcel from Prue.

"I wonder what it is," joked Sean.

"I hope it's not one of your joke books," Kathy retorted. She carefully opened the neatly wrapped red and white Christmas pudding patterned package and lifted out Barry McKnight's *Country Cookin'* book.

"Wow! Brilliant!" she said.

"Isn't that the one you hinted at?" asked Sean.

"Yes — obviously one of you listened. Very thoughtful. Thanks."

"It must have been a good offer — wish I'd known where they got it for a tenner. I hunted high and low and best price I could find was £14.99. I wish Santa had told me where the bargain price was for my sister," said Prue.

"Right, back to work for a wee while — it'll soon be time to hit Veni, Vidi, Vici. Thanks everyone for the thoughtful gifts," said Sean.

Later, in the bar Sean sat at a tiled table nursing a whiskey and ginger. The frescoed wall beside him depicted Roman ruins. Bunches of purple plastic grapes adorned a loggia overhead.

Their alcove overlooked Veni, Vidi, Vici's front entrance downstairs from where they'd waved goodbye to Kathy an hour earlier as she climbed into the waiting taxi, clutching her Secret Santa gift tightly under her arm.

"I wonder who the phonecall was from?" asked Prue.

"Maybe she has a mystery man after all!" said Jolene. "She was certainly in a rush to get away after he phoned."

"She was one happy lady for a change when she got that book earlier," said Sean.

"Not for long!" said Jolene.

"It must have been Henry," said Prue. "It's the sort of thing he'd do."

"No. He wouldn't. He likes a bit of Christmas sparkle with everything and he's a real stickler for his rules," said Jolene.

"I don't know why she's so nasty to him," said Sean.

"I know – we all love him. I think she must be secretly jealous of him organising everything so well," said Jolene sipping her glass of Pinot Grigio.

"He never says anything to her. He puts up with her. So which one of you got her the cookbook?" asked Prue.

"Not guilty. I got Henry's," said Sean.

"And I got yours, Sean," said Jolene.

"Great taste, Jolene! Thanks," said Sean.

"And I got yours, Jolene," said Prue.

"Thanks, Prue. I love them," said Jolene.

"So it must have been Henry that got Kathy's, which means Kathy must have got mine," said Prue, "but snowflake earrings and bath bombs aren't like something she'd buy me."

"Only one way to find out," said Jolene, taking out her phone. "I'll ask him."

"Hi. How's things? Meal was a great choice… Sorry you missed it… My chicken was amazing and the cranberry tiramisu was so good. And Kathy didn't complain about anything. That must be a first. Don't know what's got into her. We'll have to come back when you're better and celebrate again," she told Henry.

"Ask him!" shouted Prue clinking the ice in her glass of gin. "Put him on speaker phone!"

"How's the ankle today?" asked Jolene.

"Agony. And I can't get the hang of these crutches."

"That'll take time. I hope you're getting pampered and resting," continued Jolene.

"I am. Send me the pics of the Secret Santa gifts."

"So we've realised you broke the Secret Santa rules. There wasn't anything frivolous in Kathy's present," Jolene continued.

"I didn't break the rules. I didn't get her present. I got Prue's, and I've just broken a different rule by telling you that," said Henry laughing.

"I don't believe it! She took her own name out twice!" said Sean. "No wonder she's so pleased with herself!"

"Unbelievable!" said Jolene.

"It's sad that she didn't embrace the spirit of it. She wouldn't have spent that much on one of us!" said Prue.

"She seemed happy for once," said Sean.

"I don't think she's so happy now," said Henry.

"What do you mean?" asked Jolene.

"I don't think she'll be participating in Secret Santa next year," said Henry.

"That's a shame. That could have been good fun," said Sean.

"Once she realises we've spoken to you and have figured out she bought herself the cookbook she'll not want to hear the words 'Secret Santa' ever again," said Prue.

"I don't think she'll be showing her face round Anderson and Murdoch's for a while," said Henry.

"That's a bit extreme," said Prue.

"Why?" asked Jolene.

"It was her," said Henry.

"Yes, that's what we said. She bought herself the cookbook," said Sean.

"It was her... her car... and she was inside... driving. She knocked me off my bike."

"Seriously!" said Jolene.

"And it wasn't an accident."

"No way, Henry!" said Prue.

"The two witnesses got her registration number. Both said it was a woman driving. They said it looked like she was trying to hit me. And they both said there was something bizarre that stuck in their mind."

"What?" asked Sean.

"She can't have given all her Secret Santa gifts to the charity shop after all. They said the driver was wearing a plum pudding bobble hat."

Authors

Remco van Straten and **Angeline Adams** wrote for Verbal Magazine, Culture Northern Ireland and Fortean Times before deciding that it was time to focus on their own stories instead of writing about those of others. Their fiction is steeped in their shared love for folklore and history and draws on elements of Angeline's Co Down childhood and the northern Dutch coast where Remco grew up.

Originally from Sutton, South London, **Eddy Baker** has lived in Belfast since 2018. He has written and performed work at events around Belfast, including Tenx9 and Accidental Theatre's 'Accidental Fictions'. Eddy lives in east Belfast with his partner, Joan and their two cats, Vera and Onion. This is his first published piece of fiction.

Kelly Creighton lives in Co Down. She writes crime fiction and short stories. Her published books include *The Bones of It* and *Bank Holiday Hurricane*. *The Sleeping Season* and *Problems with Girls* are books 1 and 2 of her DI Harriet Sloane series, set in East Belfast.

Stacie Davis is a writer from Blackhill, Aghadowey and author of romantic fiction short story Ellie Bird's Greatest Regret, as well as her debut novel, *Fairytale Twist*. With her primary school teachers always describing her as a daydreamer, Stacie has been a lifelong reader, creator and enjoyer of fantasy worlds.

Sharon Dempsey is a Belfast based crime writer. The first in her new crime series will be published in 2021, by Avon Harper Collins. She is a PhD candidate at Queen's University, exploring class and gender in crime fiction. Sharon facilitates creative writing classes for people affected by cancer and other health challenges. She also writes plays and short stories.

Simon Maltman is the 'Ulster Noir' author of novels, novellas and short stories. An Amazon Bestseller, he also splits his time working as a musician and as a tour guide on his 'Belfast Noir' tour. He lives in County Down with his wife and two daughters.

Gary McKay is a speculative fiction writer from Coleraine who consumes too much tea and chocolate. He's currently working on his first novel and has had stories published in Kraxon Magazine, The Purple Breakfast Review and Tidbits. He can be found on Twitter at: @garycmckay.

Ballymoney writer, **Samuel Poots**, is working on his first novel, after receiving a General Arts Award from the Arts Council NI in 2019. When not writing he can be seen wandering the coast, muttering about dragons. If found, please send him home via the nearest post office. Find Samuel on Twitter: @pootsidoodle.

Based in Bushmills, **Claire Savage** is the author of three novels for 8-12 year-olds: Magical Masquerade and Phantom Phantasia (a duology), and The Story Forest (publishing 2021). Claire's short stories and poetry have appeared in various literary journals and she was one of Lagan Online's 12 New Original Writers in 2016/17.

Morna Sullivan has always loved stories. From Co Antrim, she is a member of the Coney Island Writers Group, Co Down and the SCBWI Belfast group. She's won a few writing competitions, has had short stories and poems published but is still chasing that elusive publishing deal.

Stuart Wilson is a published author who was born in Scotland but raised in Northern Ireland. He has been all over the world and loves to travel and runs his own business teach first aid. His hobbies include reading, writing, hill walking, sailing, rugby, ice hockey, running and Biathlon.

Jo Zebedee is a science fiction and fantasy author from Carrickfergus, best known for her novel Inish Carraig, about an alien invasion of Northern Ireland. She also runs The Secret Bookshelf in Carrickfergus.

Printed in Poland
by Amazon Fulfillment
Poland Sp. z o.o., Wrocław

66914801R00107